KOFI

and the Rap Battle Summer

*For all the children who gave me feedback
on my first draft. Thank you!*

First published in the UK in 2023
by Faber & Faber Limited
The Bindery,
51 Hatton Garden,
London, EC1N 8HN
faber.co.uk

Typeset in Garamond by MRules
Printed by CPI Group (UK) Ltd, Croydon CR0 4YY

A CIP record for this book is available from the British Library

ISBN 978–0–571–36734–4

Printed and bound in the UK on FSC paper in line with our continuing
commitment to ethical business practices, sustainability and the environment.
For further information see faber.co.uk/environmental-policy

2 4 6 8 10 9 7 5 3

KOFI

and the Rap Battle Summer

JEFFREY BOAKYE

Illustrated by Beth Suzanna

faber

Table of Contents

Don't Forget the Chicken

'Get the remote.'

Kofi and Gloria were the only two bodies in the front room. Well, it wasn't really a proper front room. They didn't live in a house. They lived in a flat on the fifth floor. But they had always called it the front room because that's what Mum and Dad called it.

Gloria was thirteen. She was the older of the two, sitting curled up on the sofa, legs tucked up under her. She was eating a slice of toast that had been buttered all the way to the sides and toasted perfectly, the way that

Kofi liked but could never get right under the grill. He always got sidetracked and looked away for too long, so it would burn. Every time.

Kofi was lying upside down in the big chair, head lolling off the edge, watching the telly upside down. If he knew anything at all about human biology, he knew that the blood had been rushing into his head for the past fifteen minutes and he'd probably get a nosebleed if he got up too quickly. He got nosebleeds a lot.

'Get the remote,' Gloria repeated.

Kofi looked at his sister.

'What did your last slave die of?'

'Not getting me the remote. Go get it.'

The remote sat quietly in the middle of the glass coffee table. It didn't dare say a word. Kofi patted his pockets.

'Hang on, I might have a spare one here somewhere . . .'

Gloria chucked a cushion at him before he could put his hand in his pocket and pull out his middle finger.

'Fine. But how about I just tell Mum and Dad that you got suspended from school again? I'm sure that'll go down well.'

Kofi slid on to the floor, sprang to his feet and grabbed the remote in one swift, panicky action.

'All right, all right! Just messing.'

She reached for it with one of her *ha-I-told-you-so*

smiles. Kofi couldn't resist. He yanked the remote out of her reach. Gloria's eyes narrowed.

'Give it. Now.'

Kofi held it up high. He wasn't yet twelve but was already starting to get taller than his sister. The next bit happened quickly. She lunged and he sprang back. Then he tripped backwards and kicked her by accident. She punched him on purpose and her side plate fell underneath his left foot. He slipped on it and fell with a crash on to the side of the table. It was one of those ones with a thick glass top that just sits on a base, not screwed in or anything. Time froze as one side of the tabletop lifted up like a see-saw. Gloria's mouth formed a perfect O, then she squeezed her eyes shut waiting for the smash. Kofi had pushed the channel down and volume up buttons by accident and the TV flicked over to ITV. *Gladiators* had just started. Gloria screamed. Kofi yelped. The table went crash. John Fashanu shouted *'Awooga!'* Then Emmanuel walked in.

'What are you two *doing* in here, man?'

Emmanuel was seventeen. He was tall and serious and worked really hard and spent most of his time trying to ignore his annoying little siblings. Today, he'd spent the afternoon working at the second-hand furniture shop and was now buried in his textbooks. He was studying biology, maths and chemistry – Emmanuel was going to be a doctor. That was the plan.

Gloria opened her eyes slowly with her teeth still clenched. The telly was blaring away while images of muscle-bound men in tiny outfits flashed up one after the other. *Jet. Trojan. Lightning. Shadow.* Shadow was Kofi's favourite. He was the only black gladiator and he had bulging triceps. His complexion was dark, like Dad's, and he would stare people out in the duel, like Mum. He never lost a duel.

'Hey,' began Gloria, looking distractedly at the TV. 'Do you think they call him Shadow because he's black?'

Kofi got up, pinching his nose.

'Oh my god, that must be true—'

'Guys!' Emmanuel interrupted. 'Look at the table!'

His long finger pointed at a huge crack that ran along one side of the glass surface. At the exact same moment, all three heads spun round at the buzz of the intercom and unmistakable click-clack of keys in the ground-floor door. Mum always buzzed ahead so they would open up when she got to their floor. She was home. Three pairs of eyes widened as everyone suddenly remembered what they'd all forgotten. The chicken!

'Don't forget to take the chicken out of the freezer and

defrost it ready for dinner.' Mum's voice played out in their heads.

'*Contenders, ready!*' Another click on the lock. '*Gladiators, ready!*' The jangle of keys through static. '*Three! Two! One! Go!*'

'Kitchen!' shouted Kofi.

The thing about spending your whole life being energetic and excitable is that you get very good at coming up with last-minute plans to get yourself out of trouble. This is why Kofi immediately ran to the kitchen and yanked the frozen chicken pieces out of the freezer, stuck together in one formidable block, before turning on the hot tap full blast and running off to the bathroom.

The thing about spending your whole life being the middle child is that you end up being the cleverest one in your family and correcting the mistakes of your idiot little brother. This is why Gloria immediately flicked on the kettle to get some water on the boil.

The thing about being the eldest is that you know exactly what will and won't make your parents explode with anger or collapse with helplessness because you've grown up seeing them with babies and toddlers running around trashing the place. This is why Emmanuel stood there looking alternately between the cracked table, the crumb-laden side plate and the slab of frozen chicken pieces, mentally working out how much trouble everyone was going to be in and for how long.

Kofi emerged with a can of deodorant and grabbed a cheap plastic lighter from a drawer next to the cooker.

'The lift is still broken so we've got a couple of minutes. Mrs Weaver is at home so she might catch Mum on the way up.'

The kettle bubbled and Kofi flicked on the lighter.

'Kofi, what are you—'

He didn't give Gloria a chance to finish.

'Stand back.'

Holding the lighter at arm's length, he aimed it and the deodorant at the floor and sprayed it fully into the little lighter's wobbling yellow flame.

WHOOOSH!

A rush of fire roared forward, making Emmanuel shield his eyes.

'The fire alarm!' he protested.

'Don't worry!' called Kofi over the flames. 'I took the batteries out yesterday to put in my Game Boy!'

'Stop! That's enough!'

Gloria waved an arm at her brother and knelt forward to see. Miraculously, Kofi's plan had kind of, sort of worked. The chicken pieces were starting to separate and almost all of the visible frost on top was gone.

'Sink.'

She hoisted the slab upwards and tossed it into the sink before emptying the kettle of water on top.

'Kofi, give it some more fire. Emmanuel, go lock the door.'

Neither boy argued. Emmanuel returned to find Gloria rummaging around in a side cupboard looking for a tablecloth. She found one and threw it to Emmanuel, who draped it gracefully over the coffee table.

'All right, everyone, look natural!' he hissed.

The trio flung themselves on to the sofas just as the rattling of keys in a lock could be heard.

The door opened. Everyone kept their eyes on the screen.

'Yo.'

They looked up. The man standing in the front-room doorway had dreadlocks, a big grin, and was definitely not Mum. Neither was the young woman standing next to him, who was wearing, Emmanuel noticed, a very short skirt.

Emmanuel jumped to his feet.

'Uncle Delroy?'

The Return of Uncle Delroy

Uncle Delroy was Mum's brother. He was older than her but seemed younger and had the exact same flash of mischief in his smile that Kofi wore most days. The one that made some teachers hesitate whenever they saw him coming.

Emmanuel could remember his uncle from when he was young. He had fond, hazy memories of being scooped up and swung around, and one time being allowed to sit next to him in the passenger seat of a flashy car. Mum had often talked about 'Uncle D' but

Gloria and Kofi had only seen him a few times. Still grinning, he let a heavy duffel bag drop to the floor with a thud and outspread his muscular arms.

'Manny! Look how *lanky* you got, man! Come here!'

Before Emmanuel had the chance to answer, Uncle D grabbed him in a big, swaying bear hug.

'Jeanette, this is my little nephew Emmanuel. But you can call him Manny,' he continued, slapping his nephew hard on the shoulder. The woman beamed a broad smile that suddenly made Emmanuel very interested in his own feet.

'*Little?*' She raised a hand to head height as if measuring him up.

Gloria and Kofi raised their eyebrows at each other. Uncle D turned his attention their way.

'And you two must be Gloria and Kofi, yeah? I haven't seen you in *time*!'

'Is that real gold?' Kofi was pointing at the bracelets and thick gold links around Uncle D's neck. Gloria gave him a look.

'Sorry, we can't turn his stupid switch off.'

Jeanette laughed long and loud and snorted through her nose. Gloria instantly decided that she liked her.

'I'm Jeanette,' she said. 'Your uncle's girlfriend.

I haven't missed *Gladiators*, have I? I watch it every week.'

She threw her head down and up, flicking her long hair forward and back, before sticking out her chest and posing with both hands high on her hips. Kofi thought Emmanuel's eyes might pop out of his head.

'Jet!' Jeanette announced, mimicking the brown-haired gladiator. 'Mind if I?'

She plopped down on to the three-seater sofa in between the two bewildered children, picking up the remote and putting the volume up. Uncle D fell into one of the single-seaters like a man who had just completed a long journey. He sniffed the air.

'You been barbecuing flowers in here?' he asked no one in particular.

'Um, yeah. I mean, no,' sputtered Emmanuel. 'Uncle, Mum didn't say you were coming tonight.'

'Nah, I didn't tell her,' Uncle D casually replied.

'*Delroy!*'

Two voices spoke at the same time: Jeanette, who couldn't believe Delroy had turned up unannounced, and Mum, who had just appeared at the door. The two women looked at each other and did that thing when two people completely size each other up in a fraction of a second. An instant later, Mum smiled warmly. She naturally liked people and Kofi could tell that she didn't have her guard up. But he felt himself sit up straighter anyway. Mum didn't mess about.

'What are you doing here?' she said softly, not so much an accusation, gliding forward to embrace her brother. Then, looking at each of her children in turn: 'And what happened to the table?'

Then she sniffed the air.

Years of experience told Gloria and Emmanuel what to do next. They both pointed straight at Kofi.

'*He* did it.'

Delroy whistled and laughed.

'You lot are cold.'

*

Kofi spent the next half hour getting in the way, trying to watch *Gladiators*, being told what to do, and counting how many times Emmanuel stole a glance at Jeanette. He was on sixteen by the time Mum asked him and Gloria to set the table for dinner. Gloria leaned in like a conspirator as they took plates and cutlery out of the cupboard and drawers.

'OK, so it sounds like Uncle D got evicted from his flat after getting in trouble with his landlord.

Something about an argument over heating and repairs or something. He was sticking up for everyone and it went a bit far. He and Jeanette are going to stay with us until they can get back on their feet. He's got a big job coming up so he can pay a bit of rent. Dad doesn't know any of this yet, but I think Uncle D helped them out back in the day. Turns out he's had a key for years.'

Kofi briefly turned his attention away from the direction of the telly.

'D'you think he'll let me borrow one of his gold chains?'

Gloria looked at her brother, sighed, and walked off with a clattering stack of plates.

Dad and the Telephone Bill

It was a bit of a squeeze but everyone managed to fit around the little foldaway table in the corner of the front room. They were one chair short so Kofi had to sit on a plastic crate turned on its side. The telly was off and Gloria had switched on the little table lamp she'd bought from Woolworths six months ago. It was the only lamp in the flat, and it cast a warm, soft glow across the crowded table.

Dinner had gone well. Kofi had only been given three warnings so far and the food had managed to stretch to feed the visitors. Uncle D was a natural storyteller and had everyone in stitches with tales of when he and Mum were young, back in Jamaica. His impression of a waddling, stick-waving Mrs Ambrose made Jeanette snort water out of her nose, which set everyone else off. Kofi knew Mum was super relaxed because, every now and again, you could hear the faint traces of her Jamaican accent. Soon, every plate was empty.

'I'm telling you, sis,' said Uncle D, leaning back and licking his fingers. 'The way you put them spices together, it's almost as good as—'

'Kentucky Fried Chicken!' Kofi interrupted.

'Almost as good as *Mama* used to make,' continued Uncle D, gently elbowing his nephew. Then to Mum: 'Make sure you teach Gloria the recipe – this stuff can't leave the family.'

Gloria cocked her head to one side.

'Just me? Uncle, uh, *hello*? It's *1994*? Boys can cook *too*?' Gloria spoke in pouts and question marks when she was trying to make a point.

Uncle D pulled his face back and raised his hands in mock defence. 'Oh, my bad, baby girl!'

Gloria pointed a finger and opened her mouth to respond, but the click-clack of the front door made everyone stop and turn. Dad must be home. He worked late on Saturdays. Mum had saved him a plate in the oven.

'That must be Dad,' said Emmanuel, starting to get up.

'Wow, you're clever,' quipped Kofi, dodging his brother's attempt at a threatening look.

Emmanuel paused, mid-rise. All six pairs of eyes were darting left and right, looking at each other in quick, rapid blinks. The sound of Dad taking off his coat and shuffling through the post could be heard from the hall. He was mumbling something about the lift still being broken. Dad was pretty mellow overall but everyone knew he didn't really like surprises. The table stayed quiet as they all wondered what he might have to say about the unexpected visitors. Everyone suddenly felt like naughty schoolkids about to get caught by the head teacher.

'Let's hide,' Jeanette whispered, making Gloria and Kofi giggle.

Mum came round first. She arched her neck and turned, opening her mouth to call into the hall. But before she could speak, in swept Dad, clutching a slip of paper in one hand and a ripped envelope in the other. He clicked the big light on and everyone squinted in the glare. The look on Dad's face told Kofi straight away that something was wrong. Dad shook the telephone bill that was clasped between pinched fingers.

'Who's been calling oh one seven one eight seven six five three six seven?'

He didn't even have to look down to read the number. Gloria's jaw stiffened.

Kofi Owns Up

'Well?'

As Dad's eyes scanned the room, Kofi eased slowly back into his chair, raising his hands behind his head in smug satisfaction. For the first time in as long as he could remember, Kofi relaxed in the knowledge that this time he wasn't the one to blame. He hadn't called oh one seven one eight seven six five three six seven, because he never used the phone. He couldn't understand how his sister could sit there for hours at a time talking pure air to the friends she would see at school the very next day.

Dad hated wasting money. For once, it was Gloria who was gonna get it. This was going to be good.

There was a moment's pause as Dad realised that Other People were at the table, and then everyone started talking at once. Mum started explaining that her brother was going to be staying for a while, Uncle Delroy started introducing Jeanette and talking about the last time he'd seen Dad, Dad started asking when Uncle D and Jeanette had arrived, Emmanuel started clearing away the plates and making his excuses and Jeanette started apologising for taking an extra piece of chicken and randomly asking if Dad was hungry.

In the sudden rush of chatter, Kofi felt a sharp kick on his shin from under the table. He scowled sharply at his sister and she widened her eyes back at him. Now, it's a well-known fact that siblings of a certain age know exactly how to communicate with each other in the presence of their parents and other adults without actually saying a word. In a film, each look would have come with subtitles:

Kofi!
What?
Tell him it was you.
It wasn't me! It was you!

Another kick to the shin.

Ouch!
If you don't say it was you, I'm telling them both that
you got suspended on Friday!
You wouldn't . . .
I would!

It suddenly fell quiet on someone saying something about paying rent, and Dad's attention pivoted back to the letter in hand.

'Well? Who made all these calls?'

The look Gloria gave Kofi could have melted holes in concrete. Kofi tightened his lips. Gloria started to speak.

'Mum, Dad, on Friday Kofi got su—'

'OK, it was me!'

Kofi glared at his sister's smug face.

Even Dad looked surprised.

'Oh one seven one eight seven six five three six seven?' He let his arms fall to his sides. 'Kofi, you really called that number forty-eight times last month? Mostly when your mother and I were at work?'

Dad was gaining momentum.

'Who is it anyway?'

Pause. Kofi waited for the universe to come and rescue

him but nothing happened. He looked searchingly at Gloria, who was now totally absorbed in a stray pea on the tabletop. He was alone.

'It's ... it's ... it's my ... my ... my girlfriend,' he managed. 'I have a new girlfriend and I call her up all the time, because ... I ... um, I miss her?'

'Aww ...' said Jeanette, putting both elbows on the table and resting her head in her cradled hands. She leaned forward and Emmanuel knocked a glass across the table.

Mum was always the cool one. She gently took the bill from Dad's hand and made a suggestion. 'Well, I think we should call this *girlfriend* right now and explain that Kofi won't be in touch so *often* any more. How does *that* sound, young man?'

'No!' yelped Gloria.

Everyone turned to look at her.

'I mean, we don't want to embarrass him, do we? *Do* we?'

Uncle D took a sharp intake of breath. He was watching the whole thing like it was TV.

'*Forty-eight* calls?' He shook his head. 'You never heard of playing hard to get?'

'Not helpful, Delroy,' said Mum.

'Just saying,' he laughed.

'We'll get this sorted out in the morning,' warned Dad. Then he sniffed the air with a confused look on his face.

'Barbecued flowers,' said Jeanette.

New Friends and Old Tricks

It was starting to get late. The adults were huddled in the kitchen, talking about something or other while the kids were left in the front room. Kofi and Gloria were sprawled flat on their fronts playing a game of Connect 4. Emmanuel was perched on the edge of the sofa, his head buried in a textbook that, to Kofi, looked as thick as the Yellow Pages.

'Your move,' said Gloria smugly, resting her chin on a cupped hand. She'd engineered the perfect two-way trap.

'Oh my god!' exclaimed Kofi, pointing suddenly. 'Look!'

Gloria turned to see what he was pointing at and her brother immediately picked up two red pieces, dropping them in at the same time.

'I win,' Kofi beamed, and was met with a sticking-out tongue from his annoyed big sister.

The adverts came on and momentarily grabbed all three siblings' attention. They were louder than the scheduled programmes. All three pairs of eyes watched as the screen showed a bunch of happy, smiling people chatting into little grey telephones with no cable attached. Out of nowhere, Gloria and Kofi spoke at the same time:

'Black person!' they said.

Emmanuel shook his head. It was a kind of ongoing game they played. Whenever a black person showed up on TV, it was a contest to see who could call it first. The TV continued showing the happy people on their phones.

'This is so fake,' said Kofi. 'I don't even know anyone with a mobile phone.'

'Kofi, you're eleven,' stated Gloria flatly.

'They're too expensive,' offered Emmanuel, looking up briefly.

'You'll be able to afford one, one day,' said Kofi, turning to face his brother. 'Y'know, when they start paying you to be in a freak show.'

He laughed, dodging the cushion that was thrown his way. Gloria couldn't help but laugh too.

'What's so funny?'

Mum emerged from the kitchen with a face that said: *Plan*. Everyone looked up. She pointed at the boys in turn.

'You two are sleeping in *here* tonight.'

*

Shortly after, Kofi and Emmanuel found themselves laying out sheets and duvets across the sofa and floor of the front room. This was going to be their new bedroom. Uncle D and Jeanette were in the boys' room with the bunk beds, Mum and Dad would stay in theirs and Gloria would keep the box room. Kofi thought it was grossly unfair, but being the youngest, he had the least say of anybody.

As they billowed sheets open and clumsily stuffed duvets into duvet covers, Kofi could hear the faint sounds of life on the estate. A few voices, cars revving in the distance, a dog barking somewhere nearby.

Soon, they were both lying down: Emmanuel on the floor, Kofi on the sofa. Kofi had put the telly on really quiet and was clicking through all four channels, one after the other. There was nothing on.

'You still haven't told me why you got suspended,' said Emmanuel. Even though there was more than six years between them, the two brothers were actually quite close, and Emmanuel knew when Kofi was lying.

Kofi sighed. He put the TV on standby and stared at the little red light in the corner.

'Photocopying,' he said finally.

Emmanuel propped himself up on one arm.

'What?'

Kofi looked at him. He didn't think his brother had ever been in trouble at school. He lay back and decided to tell him everything.

Kelvin's Big Secret

Kofi had been going to St Campions since September last year. It was the same school that his brother had gone to when he was younger, but it was nowhere near as good now as when Emmanuel was there. But Dad had insisted that all of his kids would go to a Catholic school because he thought that church schools were better than secular ones. That's why Gloria went to St Ursula's.

None of Kofi's friends from the estate went to St Campions. It was quite far away, so Kofi found himself setting off for school on his own, alongside tired-looking builders, nurses and sleepy mums and dads returning from night shifts. At first, he hadn't liked it, but he soon got used to the journey and even started experimenting with different combinations of bus, walking and train.

About a week into term, Kofi noticed another kid in a St Campions uniform who seemed to be travelling from near his estate. He was small, with short curly hair and a fair complexion, and somehow you knew he was quiet just by looking at him. He wore an oversized blazer and carried a leather satchel, rather than a rucksack like everybody else. His name was Kelvin, and he barely spoke. It took another week for Kofi to spark up anything like a conversation, and even then, it was only one-word answers.

If you saw them walking together, you might wonder why they were even friends at all. Kelvin walked with measured steps and barely said a word. Meanwhile, Kofi was like a firework that hadn't been stuck in the ground properly, spinning and yapping without a single pause for breath. The arrangement suited both boys fine. Kofi loved to talk, and Kelvin loved to listen. He was happy enough to let Kofi's voice take up all the air, like the radio being on while you did something else round the flat. And it felt good to be spending time with someone who was so loud and confident all the time. Kelvin was used to that. His mum was loud too.

Kofi liked being around Kelvin for the exact opposite reason. Kelvin was the perfect sounding board for all of Kofi's freewheeling observations and mad conversations. Kelvin didn't say much, but he knew about everything, and always gave Kofi space to lead the way.

Like his dad, Kofi was obsessed with money. But unlike his dad, he was very, very good at getting it. It was like a puzzle he could figure out with no clues: how to make money through ingenious plans. He'd already managed to save almost thirty pounds by figuring out how to get free haircuts at Fly Cutz, the local barbershop. He would deliberately ask to get his hair cut by a trainee or new starter, and Big Tyrone, the main barber, wouldn't charge him for it. This meant that he didn't get a trim every two weeks like he would have liked to, but he didn't mind if his hair was a bit picky. As long as the rudegirls on the bus didn't start cussing him out for it. (Kelvin didn't go to Fly Cutz. He told Kofi that his mum cut his hair with scissors at home.)

When Kofi discovered that his new friend Kelvin had a secret, special talent, he instantly conjured up a way of turning it into cash. It all started on the day Kelvin almost got hit by a car.

It was a Tuesday after school, which is the day of English detention. Kofi was always in English detention because he and Mr Downfield, his English teacher, hated each other. Kofi got the feeling that Downfield was one of those teachers who had instantly decided that Kofi was a bad kid. Kofi stood out from the crowd. He knew that about himself, but it seemed unfair for teachers to assume he was up to no good all the time because of it.

Kelvin was waiting for him at the bus stop, as usual, and by the time Kofi was allowed to leave, the whole school was empty and quiet. Even the mini-market on the main road had emptied of kids stocking up on sweets and crisps, perfectly timed to ruin their dinners when they got home.

There were lots of buses that Kofi and Kelvin could take, but the 16A took them closest to home without having to change. Problem was, it hardly ever came. So when you saw it, you got it.

'I hate that guy,' muttered Kofi, swinging one arm of his rucksack over his head and across his body. 'Don't you?'

Kelvin started making some mumbling sounds and gave up with a shrug.

'He always looks at me like I'm doing something wrong, even when I'm not. And then the minute I do something little, it's like all the made-up stuff in his head explodes and he puts me in proper big trouble. You see it too, yeah?'

Kelvin nodded. He had to admit that some teachers did seem to have it in for Kofi.

'S'true,' offered Kelvin quietly. 'You should b-be a bit more focused and, y'know, perfect . . . like me,' he added with a mischievous smile.

'Ah man, teachers just like you because you don't say noth— *16A!*'

Kofi interrupted himself and pointed excitedly at the open-backed double-decker bus that was starting to grumble its way up the high street. He set off at a sprint.

'Come on!'

The boys ran as fast as they could, getting ready to jump on the moving deck. Kofi leaped and managed to get on first. The conductor was upstairs so there was room on the platform. Kelvin made a jump for it as the bus lumbered around a corner.

'Kelvin!'

Neither boy realised that Kelvin's satchel was wide open at the top. As the bus swung round, it juddered and the contents of his bag billowed up into the air. Kelvin almost fell off the platform into the oncoming traffic, but Kofi just about managed to pull him to safety by a single strap.

'It's just homework, man, leave it!' shouted Kofi, wondering why Kelvin looked so worried.

Then Kelvin jumped.

The sound of car horns and screeching tyres wailed through the air. Kofi watched his friend scrabbling around for scraps of paper in the road and instinctively hopped off the platform too. The 16A rumbled away into the distance and the two boys scrambled back on to the pavement.

'What are you doing, man!' Kofi shouted. Kelvin was breathing hard and frantically shuffling his papers into order at the same time.

Kofi snatched a bunch of sheets.

'Kelvin, you tryna get us *killed* over some old homework or someth—'

He trailed off.

'Wait, are these ... ?'

Kelvin looked up at him.

'Where did you get these?' whispered Kofi, in wonder.

Kelvin breathed twice.

'I rrr-rrr – I wrrrrote them.'

Kofi Has an Idea

'These are the Cussing Matches!' Kofi exclaimed.

Kelvin nodded. Kofi was amazed. The Cussing Matches were a St Campions tradition and, as far as Kofi was concerned, one of the only reasons worth going to school in the first place. Every lunchtime, groups of boys from Years 10 and 11 would gather behind the refectory and do battle. It was verbal warfare of the highest order, contenders going head-to-head with the worst insults they could think of to a live audience who could make you or break you. The winner was decided by crowd reaction. No one was safe and no topic was out of bounds. You could talk about people's clothes, their shoes, their haircut, even their mum. The only rule was to be funnier than your opponent and get that crowd reaction.

Cusses could get serious too – Kofi had seen more than a few people lose their cool and start throwing punches, which automatically meant that you had lost. If you couldn't come back with a cuss and had to resort to violence, you were out.

It was an unspoken rule that lower year groups, known as the youngers, weren't allowed to take part. A few Year 8s had started their own side league but it was small time compared to the 10s and 11s. Kofi dreamed of the day that he could get the whole school cheering behind him as he destroyed some joker with a series of well-timed punchlines. But for now he just had to stand at the edge with Kelvin and the other youngers, watching the free entertainment and going 'Ooooh!' whenever something devastating was said.

Kelvin had pages and pages of Cussing Matches, every word written down in beautifully neat handwriting. Reading them back was like a word-for-word script. He'd captured lightning in a bottle. For the next ten minutes, the two boys stood on the pavement looking through line after line of Cussing Match heaven. It was a treasure trove. A gold mine of the world's funniest cusses, transcribed in glorious detail, going back weeks, months even. Kofi couldn't believe what he was seeing.

'When did you write all this?' he asked. It couldn't have been while the matches were happening – he would have noticed.

Kelvin started motioning with his hands, then tapped his temple.

'What, you just *remember* it all?' Kofi's eyes got even wider. 'There's *hours* of this stuff here. That's amazing.'

Then Kofi had an idea.

Actually, what happened is he had three or four ideas all at the same time, combining into one big lightning bolt of an idea that hit him like electricity. And all it needed was Kelvin's incredible memory for words.

*

Kofi put his plan into action the very next day. He collected up all of Kelvin's Cussing Match papers and put them in a special folder that he was going to carry with him into every lesson. Then came the hard bit. He stayed on his best behaviour for every teacher, all day long, every day. Even for Mr Downfield, his English teacher. After four and a half excruciating days of being good, it finally paid off when his form tutor, Miss Rich, chose him to run an errand to the office for her. It was the first time he'd ever been sent out of class for something good. Someone actually dropped a pen in surprise.

As soon as he was out in the corridor, Kofi stole his way towards the reprographics room, where the school photocopier was. It was strictly out of bounds for students, but he knew it would be empty during assemblies and form time. He sneaked past the admin office, ducking low beneath the glass-panelled door. If anyone caught him, he'd say that he was lost. They were well into their second term, but the excuse would probably work with one of the admin staff. Maybe.

The photocopier was a huge, formidable-looking machine. It had a giant panel full of buttons with every letter of the alphabet, all the numbers, and a few symbols that Kofi had never seen before.

He didn't have long. He'd memorised his form tutor's photocopy code after seeing her punch it into the small, slow photocopier outside the staffroom.

He carefully punched in the four-digit number.

Nothing.

Mild panic started to set in. Kofi punched the same numbers again, faster this time.

Still nothing.

He bit his lip and thought about abandoning the mission. Then he remembered: you had to press something else before the numbers. Or was it after? But there were so many buttons to choose from. What was it? The sound of a door closing made him jump, but it was somewhere in the distance. He raked his eyes over the keypad and saw a button marked 'code'. He jabbed it hastily.

The machine whirred into life.

Kofi snapped his fingers and did a quick celebratory sign of the cross. Then he stuffed four of Kelvin's papers into the feeder tray at the top of the machine, followed by a front cover he had designed himself. It had a drawing of two boys in St Campions uniform, high-tops and cool trainers, with *Cuss Bombs Vol. 1* written in large bubble writing across the top. Kofi paused briefly to admire his work before stuffing it into the feeder.

He pressed 'copy'.

In seconds the machine had sucked up all the paper and spat out a fresh copy on smooth sheets of warm, white paper, finishing with a satisfying beep. It almost looked like a real magazine. Kofi didn't hesitate. He quickly fed the originals back into the feeder tray and tapped one followed by two zeros on the keypad before hitting 'copy'.

The machine roared into life and started spitting out duplicates of the new magazine. Kofi drummed his fingers impatiently, wondering if the noise he could hear was somebody coming. As soon as all hundred copies were out, he gathered them up and darted back towards the office.

Then he stopped.

He could see someone walking at the far end of the corridor, away from him but still in sight. It was Miss Webb, the school secretary. Kofi could tell straight away from that slow, lumbering walk that she had. Rumour had it that her name was Webb because her toes were stuck together. Kofi slowed down. He had to get back quick but he also didn't want to risk having to explain himself. Then he gasped.

The originals!

He'd left the original papers in the photocopier's out tray! Without a second's hesitation Kofi spun on his heel and raced back to the reprographics room. He grabbed the stack of papers and sped back to his tutor room, hiding everything neatly in his folder along the way.

How Kofi Got Suspended

That same day, after school, Kofi got to work. He set up outside the mini-market, where queues of St Campions kids would line up and wait to be let in. The shop had a 'two at a time' policy after school, to avoid the inevitable rush of schoolboys all getting their sugar fix at the same time. Kelvin had all hundred copies of *Cuss Bombs Vol. 1* in his satchel while Kofi went up and down the line selling them for 50p each.

The response was fantastic. In less than ten minutes, they were down to their last few copies. Kids from every year group were huddling round freshly bought copies, cracking up with laughter and remembering who said what to who. Even Alexander Lacriade in Year 11 bought a copy, laughing and telling all the other scary Year 11s that the magazine 'looked like bare jokes'. Kofi pocketed all the coins and put them in the secret lining of his blazer. Some boys tried to pay with sweets, but he was only accepting cash. Soon, his blazer was heavy with gold and silver coins.

The next day at school, *Cuss Bombs Vol. 1* was everywhere. The playground was full of small groups laughing through its pages. That lunchtime's Cussing Match was bigger than ever. A small cheer even went up when Marlon Richards, the animated Year 10 who acted as a kind of compère for the event, gave *Cuss Bombs* a special mention. Kofi couldn't believe it. He'd only used a few pages of Kelvin's notes and it was already a hit. Kelvin had written dozens more. Kofi's heart skipped a beat when he realised how much money he could make.

By the end of the day, the teachers knew all about it. A few copies had been confiscated from those kids reckless enough to sneak them into lessons. There was even a special crisis meeting in the staffroom where all the St Campions teachers tried to work out who was responsible and how something like this could happen in a good Catholic school.

The next day, Kofi was called into the headmaster's office.

The headmaster was a sweaty-faced man called Mr Redge. Everyone called him Redge, no 'Mr'. He looked like a used-car salesman, or an out-of-shape policeman. You were only really meant to see him in assembly, but Kofi had already been called to his office twice this year.

'Sit down,' Redge instructed, nodding at the chair in front of his desk.

Kofi sat down. Redge was the kind of adult who made up his mind about 'bad' kids and held a grudge against them. His voice grated through the air with something that felt dangerously close to disdain. Kofi instinctively looked down, like he did when Mum or Dad was about to tell him off. He had been taught that it was rude to look an adult in the eye when you were being told off.

'Look at me when I'm talking to you!' spat Redge, suddenly fierce with anger. Kofi didn't know where to look. Redge leaned forward and Kofi could smell a blend of coffee and stale cigarette smoke.

'We know it was you,' he growled.

Kofi felt the first pangs of panic, but experience told him not to react, even a little bit. Besides, he was certain he hadn't been seen at the photocopier.

'Mr Downfield says he saw you, down by the reprographics room.'

Kofi was unable to stop himself. 'But he hates me!' he exclaimed.

'*Don't* you *dare* raise your voice in here!' warned Redge, jabbing the air in front of Kofi's face with a chubby pink finger. 'You're in enough trouble as it is!'

Kofi could feel a nosebleed coming on and raised his chin, looking at Redge down the length of his nose.

'Oh, so you wanna act the big man, eh?' said Redge, squaring his shoulders. 'Do *not* push it!'

He was red in the face now. Kofi started to worry what might happen next. He tried to speak.

'*Don't* you *dare* answer me back!' Redge hissed. 'I know it was you, *everyone* knows it was you, *you* know it was you. This school will *not* tolerate it. And don't even *think* about lying to me, sunshine! You've done that before.'

Fair point. Kofi had to admit he had.

'It's kids like you that give schools like this a bad name,' declared Redge. '*You* –' Redge pointed again with even more venom than last time – 'are suspended!'

Kofi felt a trickle of blood leave his right nostril.

'Now get out!'

Back in the Flat

'…and that was how it happened,' Kofi finished. 'The school phoned home later that afternoon and only Gloria was in. I got sent home early with a nosebleed. But she worked out straight away that I was in trouble too. And here we are.'

Kofi stopped and waited for Emmanuel to respond. The flat was almost silent now. They could just about hear low voices coming from their room, where Uncle D and Jeanette were staying in the bunk beds.

'Kofi,' began Emmanuel, turning on to his side in

an attempt to get comfortable. 'If you put half as much energy into your work as you do into getting in trouble, you'd be a straight-A student.'

Kofi shifted restlessly.

'And you know,' Emmanuel added, 'you should really tell Mum and Dad about what's happened. It's not good to lie. Night.'

Kofi put his arms behind his head and stared up at the ceiling, thinking long and hard about ... how he could get access to another photocopier.

'Night night,' he said, his eyes wide open.

The Biggest Idea Yet

The next few days were spent getting used to having two extra people in the flat. By Friday, they had worked out a system:

Mum and Dad would be up and out for work before anyone else woke up, leaving the kids to battle it out for the bathroom. Gloria would go first because boys are disgusting. Uncle D would hammer on the door while Kofi was in the shower, demanding to use the toilet after a late night out with Jeanette and their friends. Then he would drink the last bit of orange juice or use up the last bit of milk. Emmanuel would wonder why there was an empty carton in the fridge. Then Gloria and Kofi would leave the flat for school. Kofi would come back home twenty minutes later. At this point, Jeanette would be in the middle of an outrageous hair and beauty regime that spilled out of the bathroom, into the hallway and even some of the front room. Uncle D might be a) in bed, or b) up watching daytime television in a vest and jogging bottoms. Sometime between half past three and quarter past five, Jeanette and Uncle D would head out for the day. Gloria would then return from school and proceed to mercilessly order Kofi around, on the threat of telling Mum and Dad that he had been suspended. It wasn't a perfect system, but it was all they had.

It was Friday afternoon. Kofi was slouched on the sofa, watching cartoons that were technically too young for him, but actually really entertaining, when the front door clattered open. It was Gloria, cackling wildly with her best friend, Shanice, the girl at the other end of oh one seven one eight seven six five three six seven.

They fell into the hallway, all noise and limbs, dumping their bags and heading straight for the fridge. Shanice had long extensions piled up high on her head and took great pride in the baby hairs flattened in careful curls on her forehead and temples. She had big earrings that their school didn't allow, but she put them in on the way home. Gloria was usually quite reserved but when she paired up with Shanice, it was like rudegirls in training. She would unknowingly mimic Shanice's mannerisms and get a few decibels louder than normal too.

Shanice was in the middle of being very annoyed about something, which Gloria encouraged with a series of well-timed phrases like 'alie!' and 'innit doe!' Kofi rolled his eyes.

'. . . but truesay if these eedyiat yutes wanna see me switch then I'm switching then, innit?' rattled Shanice at machine-gun pace.

'Alie!' said Gloria.

The girls swept into the front room and fell on to the empty sofas, ignoring Kofi completely. Shanice flicked open a magazine she had carried in with her and carried on talking at pace. She switched topics without skipping a beat.

'This magazine is so *DRY*,' she declared, whipping through its thin pages. 'They call it *Smash Hits* but I'm telling you the songs in here are *dead*.'

'Innit doe,' replied Gloria.

'So why d'you buy it then?' asked Kofi, genuinely curious.

'Shut up, Kofi,' Gloria replied. 'And go kitchen and get me some crips, please.'

She said things like 'crips' whenever she was trying to be super ghetto. Kofi sat up, indignant.

'But you *just* came from there,' he protested.

'And you *just* got suspended from school,' she warned. Kofi sighed and dragged himself to his feet. He'd be glad when this was over.

'This your brother that got kicked out of school and you're covering for him, yeah?' Shanice didn't even look at Kofi as she spoke. 'Boy, if that was me I'd be *rinsing* him, trust. Ribena, please, darling.'

She blew Kofi a kiss that made Gloria make a face, and laughed. Kofi sloped off to the kitchen.

As he fetched the snacks, he couldn't help but listen in on their incredibly loud conversation. They were going on about *Smash Hits* magazine and how the featured lyrics section never had any good music, like ragga or hip-hop. It was always some white pop star that you heard on the radio all the time anyway. Shanice was saying how she wished they would print the words to some Shabba Ranks or something.

'Probably too much swearing though,' offered Gloria.

'Alie,' said Shanice. 'I'd blatantly buy it though.'

Pause.

I'd blatantly buy it though ...

At these words, Kofi stopped. He'd had an idea.

He raced back to the front room and snatched the magazine from his sister's hands.

'Hey!'

'Can I borrow this, thanks!'

He didn't wait for an answer and headed for the front door, stopping by his and Emmanuel's old room to pick up his brother's Walkman. He briefly looked at the tape inside. It said: *Cool Hip-Hop Mix. That'll do*, he thought, and left the flat in a hurry.

'Oi! What about my Ribena?' shouted Shanice as the door banged shut.

Kelvin's Secret Superpower

Kofi walked briskly to the next estate. He didn't want to hang around because he didn't know any of the kids from there. And it was never a good idea to be caught doing nothing on an estate you didn't live in.

His mind was buzzing with excitement about what was coming next. He always felt this way when he had a new idea – as though he was charged up by a new battery that was powering him forward. He was excited, too, to see if it would even work. Kofi loved surprising people. There was a big surprise in store for his friend.

Soon, he was at Kelvin's block.

'Kelvin!' he shouted up. 'Kelvin!'

A brief pause, then a dark window jerked open. Kelvin lived alone with his mum but she never seemed to be in, so he was always free to play out. There was still a slight nip in the air but it was brighter than it had been during winter.

'Yo, I need you down here. We're going park. Bring a pen and some paper, yeah?'

The window jerked shut and Kelvin was down in less than a minute.

'I've got a test for you,' smiled Kofi.

*

The park was empty and, like a lot of things in and around the estates, it could do with fixing up. The two boys sat at a dilapidated picnic table that Kofi was certain had never been used for a picnic of any description. Kofi handed over the Walkman's plastic headphones and pressed 'rewind' to get the cassette to the beginning of side A. Emmanuel was always very particular about his tapes and labelled everything properly in neat writing on the little card sleeve. The first song on the mix was something called 'Yo-Yo'.

'You like rap?' Kofi asked.

Kelvin shrugged. 'S-s-sort of.'

Kofi nodded. He had a theory. He leaned forward in a whisper, even though there was no one around.

'You know how you heard all those cusses and wrote them down?' he said darkly. 'From memory?'

Kelvin nodded.

'You think you could do the same thing with music? I mean, the words to songs?'

'Lyrics,' corrected Kelvin.

'Whatever, yeah. I wanna try something out.'

Kofi pushed the headphones on to Kelvin's small head and pushed play on the Walkman. The tinny sounds of a hip-hop beat came leaking through the headset, and he gave Kelvin a thumbs up.

He listened.

After a short while, Kofi clicked the stop button and motioned for Kelvin to take off the headphones, which he did slowly. Then, with a glint in his eye, Kofi slid the pen and paper across the graffiti-covered tabletop.

'Write.'

Kelvin looked at the blank sheet, then up at Kofi, shrugged, and picked up the pen. He started to write.

Kofi gazed at the sky and around at the blocks of flats that towered over him. He wondered how many people were living all cramped together like this, then thought about his estate, and all of the other estates across London, and all those people going up and down stairwells with broken lifts that smelled of wee. He wondered if any of them had ever had an idea as good as this, and let his mind imagine the glory and the money when he finally got to put his plan into action . . .

Kofi snapped out of his thoughts and looked down at the page opposite. Kelvin had written almost a full side. He was totally engrossed in his work, writing line after line in his beautifully neat handwriting.

'All right, stop there,' said Kofi. Kelvin looked up as though he didn't quite know where he was. He grinned, a little embarrassed that he had been so lost in the words.

Kofi took the page and squinted down at it. His heart quickened when he saw what Kelvin had done. If this worked . . .

Biting his lip, Kofi grabbed the headphones and put them on, rewinding the tape to the start. He hit play and booming bass notes immediately filled his head, accompanied by clattering drums and a whole crew of voices.

Up and down like a yo-yo,
I say 'Yo', and you know, here we go, so . . .

It was word perfect.

Kofi looked up at Kelvin in wonder before throwing his eyes back at the page, greedily reading all the words along with the song that pulsated through his ears.

I've got a sweet tooth, I'll see you on the roof
I never tell a lie, I always tell the truth
Hear me on the radio and see me in the booth
Batter up, batter up
I'm swinging like Ruth
But I am not a baby
Crazy? Maybe
A laser couldn't faze me and my rhymes are never lazy
I'm doing this so easy and the label's gonna pay me
My haters cannot see me like my name was
Patrick Swayze

'Who's Patrick Swayze?' shouted Kofi over the music.

Kelvin shrugged. 'Don't know.'

Kofi clicked off the music.

'Kelvin,' he said excitedly, a devious smile creeping across his face. 'It doesn't even matter. But d'you think you could do this again?'

Kofi Discovers a World of Music

For the whole of the following week, Kofi put Kelvin to work transcribing music from his brother's tape collection. He would sneak cassettes out of their old room and take them to Kelvin's park after school, along with a big pad of paper and biro he'd borrowed from Gloria's pencil case. He started asking his sister about which kind of songs she and her friends would most like to see featured in *Smash Hits*, and used her answers to guide his choices. Gloria was somewhat confused about this sudden interest in music, but was happy to tell him what was hot and what was not. Thankfully, Emmanuel was into music in a big way and had a huge collection of tapes. Hip-hop, R & B, ragga, house, reggae, soul … anything made by black artists really. Almost all of Emmanuel's tapes were bootlegs, copied off friends on to ninety-minute cassette tapes. Some were mixtapes recorded from fuzzy-sounding pirate radio stations. But as long as Kelvin could hear the lyrics, that's all that mattered. Kelvin was happy to do the work. He enjoyed writing anyway, and besides, Kofi had given him half the money from *Cuss Bombs Vol. 1*, so he knew it was worth his time.

By Friday night, Kelvin had written full-length transcripts of the following songs:

'Scenario' by A Tribe Called Quest
'What About Your Friends' by TLC
'Rump Shaker' by Wreckx-n-Effect
'Nuthin' but a "G" Thang' by Dr. Dre and Snoop
Doggy Dogg
'Real Love' by Mary J. Blige
'Jump' by Kris Kross
'Come & Talk to Me' by Jodeci
'It's a Shame (My Sister)' by Monie Love
'Caan Dun' by Shabba Ranks

'Ting-A-Ling' by Shabba Ranks
'Murder She Wrote' by Chaka Demus and Pliers
'Don't Walk Away' by Jade
'They Reminisce Over You' by CL Smooth
'Don Dada' by Super Cat
'Slam' by Onyx
'Hip Hop Hooray' by Naughty by Nature
'O.P.P.' by Naughty by Nature
'It Was a Good Day' by Ice Cube

It was a formidable list, and a powerful introduction to a whole world of music that Kofi had never met before. He found himself absorbed in the sounds and the samples, the drums and the melodies. And the lyrics. Especially in rap – the endless flow of lyrics that he sometimes didn't understand but got lodged in his brain anyway. Kofi started becoming a particular fan of Snoop Doggy Dogg, with his lazy drawl, melodic flow and bouncy rhyme patterns. The language was pretty extreme at times, so it always felt more than a bit rebellious rapping along (even quietly).

Kelvin and Kofi soon found themselves in deep discussions over topics such as who was the best rapper, Dr. Dre or Ice Cube, or what Shabba Ranks and Buju Banton were saying in their deep, growling Jamaican patois. The debates would rage on all day, before school, at lunchtime, on the way home, even while they were playing arcade games at the minicab office near school. Kelvin would go into fits of laughter watching Kofi do impressions of En Vogue and Jodeci, singing the high notes and waving his hand about.

When Kofi strolled through the kitchen one evening, whistling the tune to 'What About Your Friends', both Emmanuel and Gloria watched him in quiet amazement, letting their heads follow him to the fridge and back out of the room.

'Was that TLC?' Emmanuel asked Gloria.

Kofi popped his head back into the kitchen.

'Nope,' he said with a grin. 'It was me.'

Another Day,
Another Detention

The detention hall was cold and almost entirely empty. Every scrape of a chair leg or outstretched yawn reverberated through the dead air. Time had slowed right down, almost to a full stop, but Kofi hadn't noticed. He was engrossed in the sheets of paper spread messily in front of him, full of scribbled notes and bullet points. He was putting his magazine together.

He was so busy organising his thoughts and songs into order that he didn't even notice Mr Downfield striding towards his desk, past the scattering of kids who had found themselves in detention, like Kofi had – again.

'Homework?'

Kofi jumped in surprise. He glanced up at his nemesis and immediately started shuffling his notes away. It felt like he'd been caught doing something wrong. And weirdly, he was almost embarrassed to be seen being so absorbed in something.

'This isn't my home, sir,' he replied, stuffing pages into his blazer pockets. He couldn't resist giving a smart answer to his least favourite teacher. Mr Downfield sighed. He looked at Kofi like a puzzle he hadn't figured out yet.

'Kofi,' he began. 'I saw why you got into trouble. You were playing penny up the wall behind the refectory.'

'I know, sir,' replied Kofi, looking up innocently and placing his hands in his lap. 'I was there.'

Mr Downfield momentarily made an expression like his eyebrows and bottom lip were trying to meet in the middle of his face.

'Kofi,' he continued bravely. 'You had about a third of Year Seven lined up in groups, fully organised, with the Polembie twins acting as linesmen and Wayne Bernard collecting the coins.' He pointed out the other students in detention as he called out their names.

'Yeah, Wayne's got tiny hands and long fingernails,' Kofi blurted out in spite of himself. 'No one else can scrape up the pennies quickly enough.'

Mr Downfield pulled up a chair and sat down heavily next to Kofi.

'This is what I'm talking about,' he said, prodding the desk for emphasis. 'You're a natural-born organiser. A manager. People listen to you. And better still, Kofi, they *respect* you. Have you ever thought about that?'

Kofi paused. He didn't know quite how to respond. So he said nothing.

The clock ticked on. Downfield leaned in.

'You could be a real leader at this school, you know that?'

Tick – tock – tick.

Then the bell rang signalling the end of detention, and before the exasperated teacher had a chance to say anything else, Kofi had grabbed his bag and headed off towards the double doors, thankful to make his escape.

Paper Jam

It wasn't long before Kofi and Kelvin had enough songs to fill at least two or three editions of *Paper Jam*. That was the name they had agreed upon for the new magazine. Kofi had originally wanted to call it *W!cked Tunez Vol. 1* with a *z* at the end and an exclamation mark where the *i* should be, but Kelvin had been uncharacteristically insistent that *Paper Jam* was the better title, inspired by a teacher who couldn't get the photocopier to work at school. Because he was doing all of the writing, Kofi thought it only fair to let him have that one, and, he had to admit, it did sound better.

Kofi knew exactly where he would go to sell the magazine but he still had the problem of figuring out how to actually make the copies he needed. The school photocopier was out of the question: Redge was seriously on his case since he'd come back from being suspended. Kofi had been put on every report card under the sun and a few new ones that he was certain they'd made up, just for him. He brought up the dilemma with Kelvin during a game of *Street Fighter II* at the minicab office, one day after school.

'Maybe *you* could do it?' Kofi suggested.

Kelvin was in the middle of delivering a five-hit combo that killed Kofi completely. Then he looked at Kofi with an expression that made both boys burst out in peals of uncontrollable laughter.

'Maybe not,' sighed Kofi, wiping his eyes with his hand. 'Just thinking out loud . . .'

There weren't many kids who were reckless enough to go sneaking around using the staff photocopier to print off illegal magazines. Kelvin definitely wasn't one of them.

Round two started and Kelvin advanced with a hadouken flying kick combo that Kofi couldn't block. Kelvin was amazingly good at *Street Fighter*.

'You could trrrrrry the library,' he mumbled as Kofi dragon punched him into the sky.

'The school library?' replied Kofi, chewing his lip in concentration. Kelvin shook his head.

'No, th-the b— The big one.'

Kofi twigged. Kelvin was talking about the big public library at the top of the high street. He'd only ever been in there once before, with school back when he was in primary. Kelvin finished him off with another vicious combo.

'Allow it, man!' he said as his character died, again. Then he turned to face Kelvin. 'So they got a machine in there, yeah?'

'Yeah. B-but ...' Kelvin breathed twice. 'But it isn't fuh-frrree.'

Kofi thought for a moment.

'Hmm,' he said.

A Trip to the Library

It was Saturday afternoon.

The two boys were walking side by side through the bustling high street on their way to the library. Kofi was excited, bopping on his toes and pointing out all the landmarks that made up his little corner of the universe. He was eating one of those metre-long shoelace sweets that taste of nothing but are fun to chew. One end was in his mouth, the other wrapped around the hand that wasn't pointing everything out.

'*That's* the good chicken shop – the one that gives

you extra ketchup if you call the guy behind the counter boss,' he said, mid-chew. 'And *that's* the bad chicken shop. Pigeons fly in and they put them straight in the fryer. They think you can't tell the difference when the feathers come off.'

Kelvin looked sideways at him, the corners of his mouth twitching into a smile as Kofi's face opened up in a grin.

Kofi liked having someone to share his wisdom and bad jokes with. Being the last-born sibling, he never had anyone below him to pick on or know things about before they did.

The library was way busier than Kofi thought it would be on a Saturday afternoon. He let Kelvin lead the way as they went up the smooth stone steps of its grand entrance into the wide foyer.

Kofi couldn't help but look up. The ceilings were so high, and two wide staircases led up and around into the second of three floors. People were moving slowly around the building, leaving respectful distances between each other. There were old grey types in shabby clothes, students like Emmanuel carrying small piles of big books, and serious-faced men and women browsing the seemingly endless shelves.

'This way,' whispered Kelvin.

Kofi followed Kelvin past the front desk. He tensed up, waiting for the woman behind the desk to stop them, but she barely looked up. He glanced back as they disappeared round a dim corner. They eventually stopped in a dead end of bookshelves that towered high above both their heads.

'Now what?' said Kofi. He was already impatient. Kelvin shrugged.

'We w-wait.'

Kofi ran a finger along a row of books and looked at the dust collected on his fingertip.

'It better not be long,' he said.

*

An hour or so later, the library was ready to close. A man with a loud voice started calling out, telling people to make their way to the exit, and a few lights began to flicker off. Kofi and Kelvin had to be careful, but staying out of sight proved surprisingly easy. The library was full of corners to hide in. Soon, it was all but empty.

They waited another half hour.

Eventually, all the lights were turned out and the whole place was plunged into darkness. Kofi couldn't help but imagine all sorts of creepy things waiting in the shadows and had to shake himself out of fear, but it kept coming back. He sidled a little closer to Kelvin. His face was impassive, as usual.

'You sure it's empty?' he asked.

'Yes,' whispered Kelvin.

'So why are we whispering?' he whispered back, looking around at various ghost-shaped shadows.

They stalked carefully through the gloom, growing increasingly uncertain whether they were actually alone. There was something scary about a library at night. Kofi couldn't work out if he was more worried about being caught by a ghost or a security guard. They made their way upstairs.

Kelvin took them straight to the photocopier. It was a big one, very similar to the one in the reprographics room at school. Kelvin stooped, found the plug and switched it on at the wall. The machine shook into life with a beep and a growl that made both boys jump. It sounded extra loud in the deserted library. They smiled nervously at each other.

'Come on, let's get this done and go,' whispered Kofi.

The machine wasn't as fast as the one at school, so it took a short while to make all the copies they wanted. But soon enough, the job was complete.

'Let's go.'

They went hastily down the steps, heading for the main entrance door. As they approached it, Kofi's blood ran cold.

It was padlocked.

From the inside.

He grabbed the handle and pulled once. Then twice. Then twice again. Then a whole bunch of times in mad desperation.

'We're trapped!' he said. 'Kelvin – we're trapped.'

Kelvin's eyes were wide and helpless.

'Trapped!' repeated Kofi, pulling the door one last time in a violent rattle. 'I can't sleep in a library! There's books in here! And what happens when they find us in the morning?'

Kelvin was rubbing his jaw, clearly thinking hard. There must be another way out . . .

Both boys started looking around frantically. All the windows were out of reach and . . .

They spotted the glowing green sign at the exact same time. A little stick figure running towards a door. The fire exit! They raced towards it and turned in the direction it pointed: at another green sign, then another, and another, and another. They finally found themselves at a double door in a part of the library that was out of bounds to the general public. The door had one of those metal bars across that opens downwards with a push. A low glow came from the green sign above. Kofi and Kelvin looked briefly at each other, then both pushed the bar.

The air was immediately filled with the sound of an ear-splitting alarm ringing long and loud. The fire door opened out on to a quiet side street and cool evening air rushed into their faces. Kofi didn't wait to see if they had been spotted. He raced off in the direction of home, with Kelvin not far behind.

Kelvin's Flat

'Cool – see you in five.'

Kofi hung up the phone and reached for his jacket. He was heading out.

The library breakout had brought the two boys even closer together. It was a secret conspiracy that only they knew about, so naturally it made them tighter than they had been before. Now they had a bit of a weekend ritual. Kofi would call Kelvin to check he was ready, then come and collect him to go look at trainers in the high street.

This wasn't as weird as it sounds. Kofi absolutely loved

trainers, but obviously didn't have the money to start a collection. He dreamed of the day he would be able to buy every new trainer that came out: Nike, Adidas and Reebok, Fila, Puma and all the rest.

Kofi knew that if he could afford cool trainers, he'd be OK. He'd never really admitted it to himself but one of his biggest fears was being a failure in life. He remembered once walking past a group of tired old men sitting around the bus station, drinking out of bottles and wearing piles of old clothes. The men who you were warned to stay away from. They looked like they'd given up on life, and that life had given up on them. Seeing them had made Kofi feel a knot in his stomach. He couldn't put words to the feeling, but he knew that sadness was in there somewhere. Whatever happened to him, he never wanted to end up anything like that. Closer to home, it always gave him a little pang when he saw his parents struggling with money. He hadn't noticed it when he was younger but now he was getting older he would catch it more often. It gave him a little jolt of fear mixed with sadness, and then he would feel guilty for pitying his own parents like that.

Especially Dad. Sometimes, Kofi would find himself wishing that his dad could spot ways of making money that didn't involve doing jobs that he didn't always want to do.

Kofi's latest trainer obsession was the Nike Air Max 93, the ones with the orange-and-grey colourway. They were gorgeous. He once got a detention for drawing pictures of them all over his English book, but he regretted nothing. Every week he'd drag Kelvin into the big trainer shop on Skydale Road and drool over shoes, turning them over slowly in his hands, admiring every detail. Kelvin wasn't so fussed, but he tended to go with the flow.

Kelvin's mum worked early on Saturdays so Kofi had never actually met her. Weirdly, he had never even been inside Kelvin's flat. It was strange how that happened – how you could become good friends with someone and never spend any time in their home. It was one of the quirks of growing up in tower blocks. You hung out so much in the local area that your actual home became a bit of an afterthought.

It started raining as soon as Kofi left his block and by the time he reached Kelvin's block, it was coming down in buckets. Kelvin was out on the balcony waiting.

'Kelvin!' called Kofi. 'I'm coming up!'

He wasn't about to go walking in this weather. Kelvin nodded and went to buzz him in. Kofi scuttled to the main entrance. Moments later he was inside. The lift wasn't broken but Kofi was out of the habit of taking one, so he automatically went to climb the stairs.

Upstairs, Kelvin was waiting with a smile on his face. Kofi was drenched.

'Is it r-raining?' he joked.

'Funny,' said Kofi, following him inside.

He stopped dead in his tracks.

'Whoa.'

It's so hard to imagine what someone else's home is like that most of us never even try. Kofi had never thought to consider what Kelvin's flat might be like, but never would he have envisaged this.

Every wall was covered in a dizzying array of framed pictures, maps and prints. Posters from films and art galleries and music festivals lined the narrow corridor with names that Kofi had never heard of, like *Miles Davis* and *Jimi Hendrix* and *Nina Simone* and *Joan Armatrading*. On one wall hung a huge map of Africa with a level of detail Kofi had never seen before – dozens of countries delineated in separate colours. In and between the frames were all manner of trinkets and carvings, art made from precious metals and woven fabrics. It was like a museum. It *was* a museum.

'We can wait in the back,' said Kelvin casually. Then

he clocked the expression on Kofi's face. 'My mum c-collects stuff,' he added. 'Come on.'

They walked through and Kofi couldn't help but gasp. On almost every wall were row upon row of books, stacked on shelves that went all the way up to the ceiling. Kofi couldn't help but look up. Some of the books were displayed with their covers facing outwards. Titles with intriguing names jumped out at Kofi as he gazed around: *Things Fall Apart*; *The Color Purple*; *Africa Must Unite* . . . nothing he had read or even heard of before.

Meanwhile, other shelves were loaded with an array of trinkets and decorative pieces, sitting in piles or leaning against each other. In the corner stood a record player. It sat proudly upon a cabinet that was packed with records. Dad had a few records at home but he wasn't heavy into music. Kelvin's mum had more records than Kofi could count, so he didn't even guess. The overall effect was like a thousand journeys and a thousand lifetimes put out on display.

It had stopped raining so the boys stepped out into the grey. For a fleeting moment, Kofi looked up at the tower blocks and wondered about all the secret lives hiding away in the flats, all the surprises he would never discover, and all the things that were waiting out there to read, see and hear.

Then he shook the thought out of his head and started a conversation with Kelvin about which was better: Nike or Reebok.

A New Rapper Appears

'What song's this?' asked Kofi.

The boys were on the bus heading to school one Tuesday morning. Kofi had been checking on the latest batch of transcripts for *Paper Jam* and had stumbled across something unfamiliar. Clutching the thin sheet of paper, he leaned forward and started reading the lines of rhyme.

'*Rapper of the year right here, no calendar, my mind's animated like a cartoon character...*'

Kelvin reached out quickly to snatch the page back,

but Kofi was too fast for him and moved it out of reach. Years of sibling rivalry had given him speedy reflexes. He continued reading.

'*Flash like camera, that's not amateur, flow's so cold I should go to Canada* … Is this Tupac?' Kofi asked, holding the paper up high above his head. Kelvin leaned over the seat trying to get it back. 'Or Snoop?'

Kelvin's eyes widened in mild panic.

'It's j-just … it's just—'

Kofi suddenly realised.

'Is it *you*?' he asked with a gasp.

Kelvin sat back in his seat. He was clearly embarrassed.

'Yes,' he said quietly.

Kofi's eyebrows had risen all the way to the top of his forehead.

'Kelvin, these are good!'

It was Kelvin's eyebrows' turn to rise up. Kofi started reading again, starting from the very beginning.

'*Rapper of the year right here, no calendar, my mind's animated like a cartoon character, flash like camera, that's not amateur, flow's so cold I should go to Canada …*'

His voice was getting louder. He was getting into it.

'*Rhymes so hot it's like I wrote them with a matchstick, taking every syllable and flip it like a mattress, match this?*

Please, I don't even need to practise, every single lyric I'm spinning like acrobatics . . .'

Kofi covered his face with the piece of paper and made a noise like a kettle coming to the boil.

'I thought you was Tupac!' he exclaimed. 'How does this bit go?'

He jabbed at the page with an excited finger, adding with a laugh:

'I think I messed up the mattress bit, a bit.'

Kelvin opened his mouth to speak but shyness overcame him. The words failed to come out. Kofi didn't push it.

'Don't even worry about it, man.' He smiled, putting Kelvin instantly at ease. He smoothed out the page and started again from the top, drumming out a rhythm with his free hand while having a go at delivering Kelvin's latest lyrics. Kelvin's foot started tapping along to Kofi's rhythm as Kofi excitedly spoke through Kelvin's rhymes. The bus slowly wound its way towards school, crawling through the morning grey, the boys' laughter skipping over the hum of its heavy engine.

Brown Stew

The bathroom door swung open just as Gloria reached for the handle.

'Ugh, you didn't wee on the seat, did you?'

On Saturday mornings, Gloria liked to get in the bathroom before her brother had a chance to destroy it.

'Yep,' replied Kofi cheerfully. 'And some poo. I tried to spread it to the edges but your toothbrush didn't go that far.'

Gloria gave him a look that could crack a window and pushed past him, slamming the door behind her.

Kofi bopped into the front room, humming the tune to 'Nuthin' but a "G" Thang' on his way. He was in a good mood. *Paper Jam* was ready to go, with a carefully drawn front cover and even some illustrations to go with the lyrics.

'Why are you in such a good mood?' yawned Emmanuel, stretching his arms high above his head. Kofi usually hated the Saturday mornings that he was forced to go shopping with Mum. She would drag him around the market and the supermarket because she needed someone to help carry all the plastic bags. It used to be Emmanuel's job, until he got a Saturday job.

'No reason,' lied Kofi. Really, he was excited about putting the next phase of his plan into action. Mum would sometimes buy him a little treat if he wasn't too much of a pain when they went shopping, like a chocolate bar or a pack of stickers. He was hoping today he could be really good and get a stapler from the pound shop.

Emmanuel rose to his feet groggily and twisted into a yawning stretch, just as Jeanette came breezing through on her way to the kitchen.

'Morning, boys.' She smiled.

Emmanuel instinctively grabbed a cushion and held it over his boxer shorts.

'Smooth,' quipped Kofi, receiving a cushion to the head for his troubles.

'Tea?' called Jeanette from the kitchen.

'No,' squeaked Emmanuel, suffering from an unfortunately timed voice crack. 'I mean, *no thanks*,' he tried again, in a deep bass growl. Kofi slapped a palm across his forehead.

A loud scraping noise came from the kitchen, followed by a muffled 'oops' from Jeanette. The boys looked at each other. Jeanette was doing that thing when a guest tries to be super helpful by carrying out jobs round the house. The problem was, she was a total disaster zone. So far, she'd already broken a dish, scrubbed the non-stick off the only non-stick frying pan, and the microwave wasn't turning any more. Mum was running out of ways of telling her not to touch anything.

*

Half an hour later, Mum was gliding around the flat picking up stray items and delivering instructions like bullets.

'Kofi, go get those plastic bags.'

'Yes, Mum.'

'And don't forget your bus pass this time.'

'Yes, Mum.'

'Emmanuel, Gloria—'

'Yes, Mum?'

'Yes, Mum?'

'One of you needs to get started on the brown stew. I'll bring back some—'

'I'll do it.'

Everyone stopped and looked at Jeanette. Then everyone looked at Mum. She puffed her cheeks out in that way that means *I don't know how to tell you this, but ...*

'Oh, Jeanette, you know, I mean, you don't need to—'

'Oh no, it'll be fine!' said Jeanette brightly. 'I've made it loads. It's the least I can do after what I did to the fridge.'

'Wait, what happened to the fr—'

Mum was interrupted by the sudden appearance of Uncle D from Kofi and Emmanuel's room. Kofi wondered if he actually went to bed with all his gold chains on.

'Wha's gwannin, people,' he said with a theatrical yawn.

'Oh, I'm just telling Sonia about how I'll be making brown stew today!' beamed Jeanette.

Delroy stopped mid-stretch and his face became a picture of confusion. Then he exploded into peals of deep laughter, pointing and slapping his thigh. Clearly, Jeanette was no cook.

'I'll do it,' mouthed Gloria to Mum, who looked like she was having second, third and fourth thoughts about leaving the flat at all.

Soon, Mum was ready to go while Kofi was scrabbling around the back of the sofa looking for the bus pass he had lost, again. He found it wedged between two cushions and held it aloft triumphantly, before kissing it twice. He half turned and caught Gloria looking at him with exasperation.

'Good,' she said emphatically. 'I don't want you here taking up all the oxygen while we're making the stew.'

At this declaration, Jeanette made a little whimpering sound that clearly translated into something like 'oh no'. Gloria cocked her head to one side.

'You don't know what brown stew is, do you?' she said, after a pause.

'No, I don't,' said Jeanette, collapsing on to the sofa with relief. 'I was hoping it came in a bottle.'

Gloria shook her head playfully. 'Don't worry,' she continued. 'I'll show you.'

Jeanette raked a clawed hand through her long, straight hair. Gloria admired its length and shine. Kofi noticed Jeanette noticing Gloria noticing Jeanette's hair.

'You like it?' she asked, softly stroking her tresses over her shoulder. 'You know, I could get yours like this in *no* time. I've got all the stuff with me right now.'

Gloria wasn't sure. She knew that relaxing your hair involved all sorts of creams and chemicals that you had to leave in until the curls were gone. There was a girl in Year 11 who tried it and it went badly wrong. Rumour had it that she was left with bald patches all over her head. She wanted to wear a headscarf to school but the teachers wouldn't let her, so she got suspended and missed her mocks. Gloria looked instinctively towards her brother, who shrugged and continued rummaging around in the sofa for any other welcome surprises.

'Tell you what,' said Jeanette, springing to her feet. 'You teach me how to make round stew –'

'Brown stew,' corrected Gloria. Jeanette powered on.

'– and I'll get your hair looking like mine! Come on!'

'Kofi!' Mum's voice rang through the flat. It was time to go.

Jeanette grabbed Gloria by the hand and yanked her away before the teenage girl had a chance to respond. Kofi looked up, triumphantly brandishing a 50p coin he had found.

'Coming, Mum!' he called back.

The Boys on the Estate

Kofi struggled with the weight of the shopping as he waddled behind Mum on their way back from the bus stop. He had four bags in each hand and the thin plastic handles were cutting into his fingers. But it was worth it. He had his stapler from the pound shop, and it even came with a box of extra staples.

You knew you were close to home when you could hear the music coming from the flat on the top floor. It seemed to be playing music twenty-four hours a day, blasting out bass-heavy tunes over that whole part of the estate. Emmanuel said it was a pirate radio station. That's why it was on the top floor – to broadcast the best signal.

As Kofi and Mum rounded the corner into the estate, Kofi looked up and saw the group of boys who were always hanging out by the first-floor block. There was a little open area there from where you got a good view of anyone coming in and out of the estate. The boys were always there. They were older than Kofi, some looked even older than Emmanuel.

'Oi, Kofi,' called a tall, dark-skinned boy with a neat high-top. He looked like one of those pencils with the rubber on the end, but just a bit, well, scarier. He was called T. Kofi didn't know his full name. But T knew everybody.

Mum didn't slow down. Kofi tried to raise an arm in response but the bags were like lead weights, so he just nodded instead.

'I don't ever want you hanging out on the estate like that, you hear me?' said Mum quietly. Kofi knew from her tone that this wasn't a conversation.

'Yes, Mum,' he grunted as the music grew faint.

Five flights, three pauses for breath and one split plastic bag later, Kofi and his mother arrived at the door of their flat. Mum jiggled the key and shouldered the door open.

'Hi, Sonia!'

Jeanette was standing outside the front room with her arms outstretched in a 'ta-daaa!' K shape. It took a moment for Mum to recognise the young woman in front of her, about Gloria's height, but with long, straight hair and a face full of make-up.

Her mouth fell open. It *was* Gloria.

'Hi, Mum,' said Gloria nervously. 'D'you like it?'

Kofi clapped a hand over his mouth. He couldn't believe that for once Gloria was going to be in more trouble than him.

You couldn't see it, but at that exact moment a freight train of thoughts rushed straight through Mum's head. About how her little girl wasn't old enough to be walking around with a perm and how much older she looked with the new hair. How the bad boys on the estate would call down to her and hassle her on the way home from school. How make-up and nights out would be next and all 'the talks' she would need to have. How nice it looked and how long it would take to grow out. How to tell Delroy that it was probably time for him and Jeanette to leave, even if they were paying rent. She opened her mouth and nothing came out.

'Psych!' yelled Gloria and Jeanette in unison as Gloria pulled the wig off her head, revealing a beautiful set of tightly plaited cornrows.

Mum's mouth fell open. Then she kissed her teeth and cut both eyes. Gloria and Jeanette were doubled over in silent laughter.

'Sorry, Sonia, I couldn't help it!' she said, wiping away tears. Mum kissed her teeth again and allowed herself a smile.

'That stew *better* be good, you know,' she said, turning Gloria's head to inspect Jeanette's work. Kofi stamped his foot.

'Man, I thought you was gonna be in *trouble*,' he pouted.

Kofi Makes a Deal

The Junction was a bus ride away from Kofi's school, in the opposite direction from home. It was a huge hub where four different high streets met, alongside a string of bus stops, a train station and a whole complex of shops, including a cinema and a few department stores. Naturally, it was a major point of attraction for local schoolkids, and the perfect place for Kofi to sell his first batch of *Paper Jam*.

Kofi sat on the bus feeling the weight of Emmanuel's 20p collection in the secret lining of his blazer. He'd 'borrowed' them from the 'secret' shoebox that Emmanuel kept behind the radiator. He had no idea why Emmanuel was collecting 20p pieces, but it meant that Kofi could sell the magazine for 80p a pop, giving 20p change to anyone who gave him a pound for each sale. That was the plan anyway.

The bus pulled to a stop and Kofi headed for the exit, swinging on each pole by the crook of each elbow. He cheerfully pushed the bell a few times on his way out, earning a menacing glare from the driver that he didn't notice. He was in a good mood.

Outside, the Junction was already bubbling with activity. Kids from three nearby schools were mingling in small groups outside shops and at bus stops, or drifting like icebergs towards the main shopping complex. Kofi headed straight for the food court.

McDonald's was buzzing. Girls and boys in blazers and ties milled around in queues and at tables, laughing over French fries and fizzy drinks. *Customers*, Kofi thought to himself, and pulled open his bag at an empty table, revealing a neatly stacked pile of photocopied pages.

Twenty-three minutes later, Kofi had sold precisely zero copies of *Paper Jam*. It wasn't for lack of effort either. He'd circled every table, scanned every queue, turned on as much charm as he could muster, but nothing. No one seemed interested in buying a black-and-white photocopied magazine from some kid in Year 7.

'*What* are you doing?'

Kofi looked up from his slump at a corner table and pulled his chin away from his cupped hands. The girl who stared down at him was chewing a piece of gum furiously and wore big hoop earrings.

'Shanice?' said Kofi with a tilt of the head.

'You're Gloria's little brother, innit?' She pronounced none of her *t*'s. 'I thought it was you, innit. Why are you running around here tryna sell paper to people? Don't you know no one's tryna listen to a little yute like you?'

Kofi was too tired to argue. 'It's a magazine,' he explained wearily.

'Lemme see.'

Shanice extended a palm in a way that meant no wasn't an option. Kofi handed over a copy.

Shanice chewed and pouted while flicking through the pages through half-slit eyes. Then she slowed down.

'You made this?'

Kofi nodded. She slowed down even more and leaned forward to read a particular page.

'Rah . . .' she said quietly. 'You got Shabba in here.'

She snapped to attention, looking up so sharply that it actually made Kofi jump.

'I can't lie this is actually not dead, you know. How much you tryna sell this for?'

'Eighty p,' said Kofi. 'If people give me a pound, I've got twenty p's for change.'

He shook his blazer. Shanice pursed her lips.

'All right, gimme them then.' The last two words sounded almost identical and she pronounced them like they started with a *d*. Kofi stalled.

'Wha—? No way.'

Shanice persisted.

'Look, I could get rid of these in *no time, trust*. I know all these kids, you get me? My cousin goes Whilomena's and I got bare friends at South Tech. I could sell these quick time, man.'

She spoke so fast that Kofi was still processing the first sentence by the time she had finished the third.

'Just gimme like fifty per cent and I'll get it done. And make it a pound, man, like, what's the point in all them twenny ps.'

Kofi blinked twice.

'*Half*,' she said, rubbing her thumb and forefingers together, indicating money. Kofi's face started to twist into refusal.

'Listen, have I even got time to be dealing with some pickney though? You want to sell these or not? My chips are getting cold.'

*

Fifteen minutes later, Shanice had:

Sold all but three copies of *Paper Jam*.

Come up with a plan to photocopy more at her school.

Arranged to get new material off Kofi at the end of the week.

Started giving him his instructions as they walked their way through the complex, rucksacks heavy with a shared jangle of pound coins.

'...so make sure you don't write it too small next time, and keep it off the edges so that the copies don't cut off any of the words, yeah?'

'All right, *Mum*,' replied Kofi sarcastically, ducking.

'I beg you don't get rude,' said Shanice with a scowl.

Soon they were out by the bus stops. It was time for the unlikely duo to part company. Kofi turned to face Shanice and extended a straight arm.

'Nice doing business with you,' he said smartly.

Shanice pulled her chin into her neck and folded her arms. Then she softened.

'You're all right, Kofi, you know – for a Year Seven boy . . .'

Then, thawing slightly, she slowly extended a hand. She was starting to like this k—

'Psych!' shouted Kofi, and pulled his hand away, putting the thumb to his nose and waggling his fingers. Shanice's eyes widened and Kofi took off at a sprint, rucksack swinging side to side.

'Watch when I see you next time!' called Shanice after him, but all she got back was a cheeky wave.

Uncle D vs the Gladiators

'*Awooga!*' yelled the excited TV presenter.

'What does that even mean?' asked Gloria, to no one in particular. It was Saturday night and *Gladiators* had just started. Dad had had a late shift on Friday so he was home for a change, sitting with Mum on the three-seater. Gloria was curled up on one of the single-seaters and Jeanette was looking in every wrong drawer for the cutlery. Kofi was stretched out on his belly playing *Tetris* on his Game Boy. Emmanuel was out.

'No idea,' muttered Kofi, briefly glancing at the screen.

'He looks like you though. You know, from the ugly side of the family.'

Gloria looked at her parents as if to say, *Well?* Mum shrugged and folded a leg underneath her.

'Well, he ain't talking about me,' she said with one raised eyebrow.

'OK, that's the takeaway ordered.' Uncle D emerged from the hallway with a takeaway menu in his hand. He was treating everyone to a Chinese, partly to make up for what Jeanette had done to the veg trolley, partly to make up for Jeanette's recent attempt at spaghetti bolognese. He stopped and stared at the screen.

'I would *mash* this up,' he said, looking at the Lycra-clad gladiators flexing their muscles and smiling at the cameras. 'Sonia, you know how good I was at athletics back at school. There weren't nobody beating me!'

'Even Shadow?' asked Kofi, tapping buttons on his Game Boy.

'Which one's he?' asked Uncle D.

'The black one,' said Gloria and Kofi in unison.

Shadow flashed up on the screen, gripping a big stick with huge pads on either end and staring down the camera.

'That man is *definitely* Ghanaian,' said Dad. 'We have the exact same physique.'

Mum raised the other eyebrow. 'Do we?' she said.

'Uncle Delroy,' said Kofi, turning away from the television, 'do you really think you could beat Shadow in the duel?'

'Of course!' exclaimed Delroy, punching the air with a flurry of left and right fists.

At that point an information screen popped up with details of how to apply to be in the next series of *Gladiators*. It had an address, some dates and a telephone number.

'Hmm...' said Uncle Delroy.

'Coinboy'

'Your uncle's going to be on *Gladiators*?'

Leroy Simpson was stuffing crisps into his mouth and bits were spraying all over the place while he talked.

'Swear down?' he asked again, pushing another fistful of crisps into his face.

'Swear down,' replied Kofi.

Kelvin said nothing. He and Leroy would never have been friends normally, but they both knew Kofi so ended up hanging out that way.

It was after school and the three boys were heading to the minicab office after yet another detention. This time Leroy had scrambled a 50p coin at lunchtime and caused a pile-up outside the canteen. Mr Redge had seen Kofi laughing so he got detention too, even though there must have been more than thirty boys doing the same thing. The head teacher had a knack of seeking him out that way.

'Boy, if he gets Shadow in the duel he's gonna get *destroyed*,' said Leroy, licking his fingers.

Uncle Delroy had applied for the show using Mum and Dad's address and the letter had somehow come back in Dad's name. He only had an audition but he had spent the whole week telling anyone who would listen about how he was going to take on the gladiators and win. Kofi was excited, and already planning the sign he was going to make to hold up in the crowd.

The three boys approached the minicab office and slowed to a stop.

'You got the coins?' asked Leroy, chucking his crisp packet on the ground.

'Yeah, man,' said Kofi, pulling open his rucksack. Inside were two plastic bags, each about a quarter full of carefully prepared coins.

'Come on then,' said Leroy, and they headed into the office. Kelvin hung back and briefly looked around. Then he picked up Leroy's crisp packet and followed them in.

The office was already bustling with kids in St Campions uniforms. Mainly Years 7 and 8, with a few 9s here and there. It was small, but Leroy and Kofi still had to push their way to the row of arcade machines at the back.

'Yo, all right then, anyone playing, come get your coins!' announced Leroy over the chatter. 'We're starting in *five*.'

He held up five chubby fingers on one hand.

'Kels *the Reloader* is taking names over *there* and then come get your coins off *Coinboy* over here,' he called out, pointing to Kelvin and Kofi in turn. He loved making up nicknames.

It was a *Street Fighter II* tournament. Leroy and Kofi had set it up a couple of weeks back when they were litter-picking during PE detention. The rules were simple: you paid one pound to enter, then there were heats, elimination rounds and finals. £10 grand prize. The problem was how to pay for all the goes needed to play a full tournament. *Street Fighter II* cost 50p a turn, which meant that running a full tournament would cost hundreds of pounds in total. But Kofi had a solution.

See, there were different ways to get free goes on the arcades, and Kofi knew them all. Method one was *the sandwich*. It was a fiendish trick. What you did was take a single penny and a single five-pence piece and stick them together with a piece of chewed chewing gum. If you got the thickness just right, an arcade machine would think it was a pound coin and you got one pound's worth of goes for 6p. The other method was the *cover-up*. For this one all you needed was a 10p piece and some tinfoil. You covered the coin in the foil and by carefully moulding it into seven sides, the unknowing arcade machine would treat it like a 50p.

Kofi had a whole bag of sandwiches and a whole bag of cover-ups, ready to distribute among the competitors. In a matter of minutes, Kelvin had written everyone's name in a red exercise book and they all had a handful of Kofi's trick coins. Leroy called for attention by raising both hands.

'Let the games begin, innit.'

An excited cheer went up. No one noticed the high-top at the back watching Kofi intently.

The Rapper of the Year

The next few weeks were a dream. Kofi and Kelvin were producing regular new editions of *Paper Jam* and Shanice was selling them by the bagful down at the Junction. She would meet Kofi at McDonald's and slide his half of the profits across the table. Then he would meet Kelvin at the picnic table and give him his share.

Meanwhile, the *Street Fighter II* tournaments were gathering momentum. Even some Year 11s had started turning up. Kofi and Leroy had upped the prize money to £25 for the winner and £10 for the first runner-up. For a pound to play, it was too good an opportunity to pass up. Soon enough, even kids from other schools started turning up, forcing the boys to run two tournaments at a time.

Kofi felt like he was riding on rails. Everything was going smoothly and all the pieces of his life were falling together, like a well-played game of *Tetris*. He felt proud of himself too, for turning ideas into action. He didn't need a teacher, or his parents, or anyone to tell him he was doing well. He could feel it for himself.

'This is brilliant!' said Kofi on the way home from school. He was jangling his blazer and making all the coins jangle in the hidden lining. 'We're rich!'

He leaned over to nudge Kelvin with his shoulder, but Kelvin pulled away. Kofi made a face.

'What's the matter with you?' he asked, genuinely confused. Kelvin was getting his fair share of the money too. He should be happy.

'You sh-shouldn't be showing it off l-like that ...' murmured Kelvin quietly, looking left and right and over his shoulder. 'You don't w-w-want to get caught with all this money...'

He took a deep breath and continued.

'... E-e-especially with so many kids frrrrom other schools coming to the t-tournments t-too.'

Kelvin exhaled with the relief of having said so much in one go. He never usually disagreed with Kofi like this. Kofi tried to laugh it off.

'Oh, come on, man, it's all good! I know how to stay safe out here. I've got it under control – trust me.'

Kelvin pursed his lips and gave a look that made Kofi suddenly feel very silly.

'Come on,' continued Kofi, a little hesitantly now. 'Chicken and chips. On me.'

Kelvin's eyes looked up and around.

'S-sorry, man,' he began. 'I need to be getting home.'

He started walking and, after a pause, Kofi followed. Both boys in complete silence.

*

It was a Thursday after school and the boys were at the dilapidated picnic table, making the most of the last of the good weather. Leroy didn't live anywhere near Kofi and Kelvin, so it was just the two of them. Kelvin would never say it out loud but he much preferred it that way. Kofi had arranged for them to meet up. It wasn't particularly warm out, but the boys were both eating ice lollies that he had bought from the off-licence near the estate. Kofi didn't like to splash his money about, even on little things, but today was a special occasion. He had a plan.

'OK, here's what we'll do,' he began, chomping into a bright orange lolly on a stick. 'I'll start by drumming out a beat and it'll be easy for you to carry on. I'll start off slow, so you don't have to rush.'

Kelvin took a tiny bite of his thin ice pole and nodded, but he really wasn't sure.

Kofi had decided to find a way of getting Kelvin to rap his own lyrics. It was a nice idea but Kelvin couldn't see it working. He just couldn't get his words out quick enough, no matter how slow they went.

'Here,' said Kofi, producing a crumpled piece of paper from his blazer pocket. 'It's the *acrobatics* one.'

He thrust it in Kelvin's direction. Kelvin took it nervously. He could feel his chest tightening and his throat starting to seize up already.

'Ready?' asked Kofi, with an encouraging nod.

'Y-yeah,' came the mumbled reply.

Kofi started drumming out a slow, funky rhythm using the sides of his fists.

Kelvin opened his mouth to speak. It was quiet, apart from the faint background noise of life on the estate and the low hum of the streets beyond.

Kofi widened his eyes to motion for Kelvin to start.

Kelvin's mouth opened wider. Kofi started mouthing the first line: *Rapper of the year, right here, no calendar . . .* Kelvin licked his lip and swallowed. He had a natural sense of rhythm and could feel the next bar coming up. *Rapper of the year, right here, no calendar . . .*

Three. Two. One.

Go.

. . .

Kofi slowed down ever so slightly in anticipation of Kelvin's volley of rhymes. This was it.

. . .

'R-rrrr-rrra . . .'

Kofi stopped drumming. Kelvin looked down at the scratched surface of the old picnic table. He had really wanted it to work this time.

'Sorry,' he whispered.

Kofi looked at him. He'd never had a younger sibling but suddenly knew what it meant to be the big brother.

'Don't worry about it, man,' said Kofi softly. 'We'll get you rapping one day, I promise.'

Kelvin smiled weakly and gave a little half shrug.

'And if we don't, you can just write them for me and I'll become the millionaire instead.'

'You wish!' replied Kelvin, looking up. And both boys beamed, smiling in the afternoon sun.

Kofi Makes a Big Decision

Soon Kofi found himself with more money than he could fit into the secret lining of his blazer. He took it to Mr Ambrose, the grey-haired Trinidadian man who ran a little shop-hut on the edge of the estate. He'd ask Mr Ambrose to exchange his coins for five- and ten-pound notes.

'Where you get all dis coin, boy?' Mr Ambrose asked him one day.

'School project,' replied Kofi.

'Hmm,' said Mr Ambrose. But he didn't complain.

Getting all that change saved him a trip to the bank. Kofi now had a collection of banknotes that he put in an envelope and stored carefully in a secret hiding place at home.

One day, after school, Kofi and Kelvin were walking towards the bus stop, sharing a bag of sweets. Kofi was re-enacting an epic *Street Fighter II* battle between two Year 8s, both fighting as Ryu in a tournament final. He was dragon-punching the air and making all the sound effects. When he paused for breath, Kelvin interrupted.

'I-I-I don't think we should d-do the . . . t-tournaments any mmmmore,' he said.

Kofi looked at him, fist still in the air.

'Why not?'

Kelvin opened and closed his mouth, and sighed.

'It's it's ju-huh, ju-huhst too rrrisky,' he managed. 'There's p-p-p-people we don't . . . we don't know there.'

He was talking about the boy with the high-top, who he had noticed lurking in the back of the arcades at the last few *Street Fighter* tournaments.

Before Kofi could reply, Leroy emerged from the mini-market clutching a family-sized packet of crisps and 1.5 litre bottle of cola.

'Wha gwan, *Coinboy*,' he said, touching fists with Kofi. He ignored Kelvin completely. 'You good?'

Kofi didn't hesitate.

'Kelvin thinks we should stop doing the tournaments,' he said, pointing a thumb in Kelvin's direction.

'What?' said Leroy, confused. 'What for?'

'He thinks it's getting too *dangerous*,' answered Kofi, not giving Kelvin a chance to reply. Kelvin looked at his shoes.

'Don't listen to this fool, man,' said Leroy with a snarl, ripping open his bag of crisps. 'I don't know why you brung him in anyway.'

'D-don't call me that,' said Kelvin, quietly.

'Why?' said Leroy, taking a step towards him. 'W-w-w-w-what are you gonna do about it?' he mocked, threateningly.

There was a pause as none of the three boys said anything. A pigeon pecked around the litter at their feet. Kofi started to feel hot in his chest. But he didn't say anything.

Leroy broke the silence.

'I'm going Junction,' he said to Kofi, still looking at Kelvin. 'Come we go. This *wimp* can stay here, innit.'

Kofi looked at Leroy, then looked at Kelvin. Then back to Leroy.

'Yeah, I'm coming,' he said, slowly taking a crisp out of Leroy's packet. He gave one last pleading look to Kelvin.

Come on, man, his eyes seemed to say. *Just come with us. It'll be fine.*

Kelvin didn't move, unable to speak. Kofi was torn. He had become good friends with Kelvin – he was maybe even the best friend he'd ever had – but Leroy was drawing him in. Leroy and Kelvin were so different in so many ways, oil and water really, and Kofi wished that somehow they could become friends. But it was a useless thought because obviously it just wasn't going to happen. The moment hung in the air. It felt like a crossroads.

'You coming or not, man?' Leroy snapped at Kofi, impatiently.

Kofi opened his mouth to say something. It was a choice between being cool and being loyal, and at eleven years old, he hadn't yet figured out which was more important. Kelvin looked at him, pleading silently for him to stay.

Sorry, Kels, thought Kofi. And he bopped off with Leroy, leaving Kelvin standing on his own.

Money, Mistakes and Missing People

With all his new money, Kofi eventually took Kelvin's advice and started being extra careful in and around the estate. He began to leave for school early and aimed to get home before it was too late. He'd heard stories of youngers getting mugged on the way home from school and he knew that carrying all those coins around would get him in serious trouble, sooner or later. He felt guilty about what had happened with Kelvin, but was enjoying making so much money. Kelvin had stopped coming to the tournaments and Kofi took on the job of taking names and keeping score. He was terrible at it and more than a few arguments were caused by mistakes he made.

He wished Kelvin was still around. He wished he could say sorry for what had happened with Leroy too. He wasn't always the most thoughtful person and, truth be told, he wasn't used to having a proper friend. It was only now, after everything was over, that he realised how badly he had messed up. It made him feel so rotten that whenever he thought about it, walking home on his own, he would scrunch his eyes shut and kick at the ground in frustration.

Then Kelvin didn't turn up for school.

It was only one day at first. But that became two, then three, then a whole week, with no sign of him anywhere. Crazy thoughts of Kelvin being caught for his money and grabbed by shadowy figures in alleyways kept creeping through Kofi's mind. He even went to Kelvin's block and called up to his flat after school, but there was no reply.

He brought it up with Leroy one lunchtime.

'What you stressing for, man?' said Leroy, reaching into his inside pocket and pulling out a whole burger that he'd sneaked from the canteen. 'He's probably just off sick, innit.'

He took a huge bite of burger.

'Or dead,' he added, laughing through a full mouth.

'I'm serious, man,' said Kofi, scanning the playground for Redge. 'What if he's been got?'

Leroy took another monstrous bite.

'Then you're *next*, rudeboy,' he laughed.

*

Without Kelvin, *Paper Jam* ground to a halt. Kofi had a go at writing up some lyrics from Emmanuel's latest mixtape, but he couldn't write neatly enough and definitely didn't have the patience for all the pausing and rewinding he had to do to hear each line.

'What's this?' asked Shanice with a look that could make a dog apologise. They had met at the Junction and Kofi had just presented her with his attempt at the latest *Paper Jam*. It wasn't very good.

'It's not very good,' he said sheepishly. Shanice threw it back at him.

'*Nah then,*' she replied, sarcastically. 'You're lucky I don't box you.'

Kofi's face fell.

'Listen,' said Shanice with a sigh. 'You're annoying, and short, but you made something good here –'

Kofi looked up slowly as he realised Shanice was paying him a compliment.

'– and you know how to make money, clearly. It's a skill, innit.'

Kofi's face broke into a smile.

'I suppose I am a bit of a genius, aren't I . . .'

Shanice rolled her eyes.

'Look, you little bighead. I'm just saying, I rate what you've done. *Paper Jam* is sick.'

They both looked at Kofi's latest offering.

'*Was* sick,' Shanice corrected herself. 'Let's get it back to how it was, man.'

Kofi scratched his head. Without Kelvin, he didn't know how that would be possible.

Caught

The bus stopped twice to change drivers, so by the time Kofi got near his estate, it was starting to get dark.

The estate was a different place at night. It suddenly had more corners and shadows where threatening shapes could lie in wait. Kofi decided to walk the way home that would keep him near the main road for longer, but he'd still need to leave the safety of a busy road eventually, just to get to his block.

He quickened his pace as he got further from the

main road, unable to stop himself thinking about Kelvin getting beaten up – or worse – by scary, older kids. The sound of the pirate radio station drifted through the air, adding a sense of menace to Kofi's journey. It was quiet, just a few kids playing out; no one that Kofi knew well. No one he knew at all really. It suddenly dawned on him how isolated he was out there, how alone he felt and how he wished he knew a few more people. He was vulnerable. The streets were dangerous and he felt like a target. He put his head down.

'Oi, Kofi.'

The flat monotone of T's deep voice made Kofi's heart skip a beat. He looked up. It was T, flanked by two of his friends. One of them was smoking. And the other, a heavyset youth with a deep squint, was carrying a satchel that looked just like Kelvin's.

Kofi's blood ran cold.

It was *Kelvin's satchel.*

'Kofi. Come for a second.'

T advanced slowly. Like a spider moving towards a fly that was already caught on its web.

Kofi stopped walking.

'Ay, just come, man,' the friend with the cigarette

said. There was a note of aggression in his voice. Kofi took a step backwards.

'I-I—'

Then he turned on his heel and sprinted off in the direction of home.

Kofi's Great Escape

The next morning, Kofi peered out of the front-room window, taking care not to ruffle the net curtains too much. There he was. T's friend, the one who had been carrying Kelvin's satchel. He'd been there all morning. Kofi had checked from the small window in the bathroom and, yep, there was T's other friend, the smoker. He didn't have to go out to the balcony to know that below his block would be T himself. They were waiting for him.

Mum, Dad and Emmanuel were already out and

Uncle Delroy wouldn't be up until Kofi had left for school.

'Gloria, I need your help.'

Kofi was desperate.

'No, you need help, full stop.'

'Gloria, I'm serious,' he pleaded.

'I'm not doing your homework, Kofi,' she said. 'Even if I write with my left hand I can't get the handwriting bad enough.'

'It's not that,' Kofi explained. 'There's some boys from the estate waiting to get me and I can't stay home off school. *Please.*'

Gloria could see that her brother was genuinely panicked. She softened slightly.

'You're gonna have to tell Mum and Dad,' she said, making Kofi wince.

'That doesn't help me *now* though!' he bleated.

'All right, then I'll walk with you,' she offered.

'Oh yeah – being protected by my big sister, that'll work.'

Gloria didn't have any time for Kofi's sarcasm and raised both hands, starting to leave. Kofi panicked again.

'Wait! Sorry! I'm an idiot!' he said.

'At least we agree on *one* thing,' replied Gloria.

'Anyway, whoever these boys are, I'm guessing they wouldn't start on a girl.'

Girl.

Girl.

A light bulb flashed up above Kofi's head.

Gloria had just turned on the light switch.

'Jeanette!' said Kofi excitedly. 'Do you still have that wig?'

*

Five minutes later, Jeanette, Gloria and Kofi were knee deep in the process of transforming Kofi into a teenage girl. Jeanette had successfully attached her wig to Kofi's head using a surprisingly complex series of hair clips. Gloria had dug out an old white school shirt, grey skirt and lower school tie. After a good laugh at how dry Kofi's legs were, Gloria and Jeanette decided to put him in tights, which he pulled all the way up over his boxer shorts.

On his face, Jeanette smeared a puff of brown foundation on each cheek and his forehead, before carefully applying a thin swipe of mascara on his eyelashes. She leaned in close.

'Your eyelashes are gorgeous, hun ...' she whispered, millimetres away from his face.

'Thanks, hun,' Kofi whispered back.

They stood Kofi in front of the full-length mirror in Mum and Dad's room and took a step back.

'Wow,' said Kofi. 'I look like a girl.'

Gloria glanced at the clock.

'Come on,' she said. 'We need to go.'

Kofi grabbed his rucksack and double-checked that he had his own clothes in there. Getting stuck as a girl all day would *not* be a good look. Gloria was already ready to go. He looked up and met the eyes of Uncle D, who had just emerged from his room.

'Oh, sorry, princess,' said Kofi's uncle, not recognising his nephew.

'Uncle, it's me,' said Kofi, flicking the wig away from his eyes. '*Kofi.*'

Uncle D stopped in his tracks.

'Bye, Gloria! Bye, Kofifi!' laughed Jeanette. Uncle D scratched his head.

'Long story,' said Kofi as Gloria pushed him out the door.

*

The minute Kofi was outside in the estate, he started having major doubts about the whole plan. There was no way he could pass for a girl, he thought, scanning the concrete walkways. Someone from T's crew would spot him for sure. And the training bra he was wearing was already starting to get really uncomfortable.

'Just calm down,' hissed Gloria quietly, while Kofi twisted a thumb into his bra strap.

'This was a stupid idea,' he hissed back. 'I should just go b—'

Too late.

There up ahead was T, and he was walking slowly towards them.

Kofi nervously smoothed down the front of his skirt.

'Is my hair all right?' he whispered to Gloria. 'Gloria?'

She was already walking off towards her bus stop. She turned with a devious smile, blew her brother a kiss and waggled her fingers to say 'bye', before disappearing round a corner.

T drew nearer. Kofi instinctively threw his gaze to the ground. And then something curious happened. As they neared, Kofi half looked up and accidentally caught T's eye. Kofi held his breath, waiting for the attack. But T immediately looked away. He hadn't recognised him.

The disguise had worked!

T didn't know it was him!

In fact, Kofi couldn't be entirely sure but T actually looked a bit, well, *nervous*.

They were just about to pass each other and Kofi decided to take the biggest risk of his life so far. He looked up. Then, holding his gaze just as they passed, Kofi smiled and waggled his fingers at T in the same way that Gloria had just done.

And T looked at the ground.

Wow, thought Kofi, as he pulled a wedgie out of his tights. *Being a girl is* really *interesting.*

Disguises and Surprises

Kofi got off the bus, tugging at various different undergarments he was wearing and wondering how his sister could put up with being so uncomfortable all of the time. There were boys in St Campions uniforms everywhere, but no one reacted to him at all. Across the street, Kofi spotted Leroy with a group of boys from Years 7 and 8, talking loudly and jumping all over the place. He very nearly raised a hand to call over, but caught himself just in time. Leroy glanced over but looked right through him.

The disguise really *did* work.

It was almost time to go in. If you were late for registration it was instant detention, so Kofi had to move fast. There was a cafe on the high street that he knew had a toilet in it, but you had to buy something to use it. The plan was to go in quickly, buy a chocolate bar, ask to use the toilet, change, eat the chocolate bar, then run back to school before the second bell.

He skipped down the street towards the cafe.

He skidded to a halt.

His heart sank. It was closed. Shutters down, everything. Spinning, he looked around frantically for an alternative. Nothing. Everything was closed. There wasn't even a phone booth he could use. He would have to find somewhere else – fast – or buy himself more time – now.

Kofi blew a lock of hair out of his eyes and raced back towards school. He had a plan.

In minutes, he was at the front desk. Kids were filing past on their way to lessons and teachers with big voices were saying good morning and telling everyone to tuck their shirts in. Kofi coughed for attention.

'Yes?'

It was Mrs O'Riordan on the desk. She was a round-faced woman in spectacles who was at least seventy per cent cardigan. Mornings were her busiest time of day, so she didn't have time for niceties.

'Um, hi,' began Kofi. 'I've got a message about Kofi Mensah? He's ... he's going to be late into school today. He had a nosebleed – or something.'

Mrs O'Riordan looked at him over the top of her glasses.

'And you are?' she asked.

Kofi hesitated.

'Um, I'm my sister ... I mean, I'm his sister. Gloria.'

Mrs O'Riordan wrote something down on a piece of paper. Kofi peered over.

'He'll be about twenty –' he pulled another wedgie out of his tights – 'maybe twenty-five minutes.'

Then he remembered that period one was English with Mr Downfield, his worst teacher.

'Actually, I don't think he'll make it in for period one at all,' said Kofi with a flick of his hair.

'OK,' replied Mrs O'Riordan with another scribble. 'Thanks, dear.'

*

Outside, Kofi allowed his walk to slow to a casual stroll. He'd given himself a bit of time, and it had been a busy morning.

There weren't any schoolkids around now – the last of the latecomers had gone in ages ago. There was a slight chill in the crisp morning air, and Kofi was suddenly very grateful for his thick warm tights. They were better than trousers.

Lost in thought, it took him a moment to recognise the boy sitting at a bus stop across the road.

He snapped out of his thoughts and squinted. Then he gasped.

It was Kelvin. He was sitting next to a woman with a brightly coloured headscarf piled high on her head.

And he wasn't in school uniform.

A bus suddenly pulled up at the stop, completely blocking Kelvin from view. There were a handful of people waiting, so the bus didn't move straight away. Kofi took his moment. He glanced left and right, then darted across the road, heading for the bus. Kelvin had already got on by the time Kofi joined the queue. Kofi jumped on behind a woman with short blonde hair and scanned the lower deck for Kelvin.

Nothing.

He must be upstairs, thought Kofi, and made for the stairwell as the bus chugged away.

Upstairs was almost empty. There was Kelvin, near the middle, gazing out of the window. The woman with the headscarf was sitting next to him, talking with animated hands. Kofi hurried past them both and sat near the back. This was usually where the rudeboys and rudegirls sat. Normally, Kofi wouldn't dream of sitting there, but everyone was at school, so it was safe. He sat down, wondering what to do next, keeping his eyes on the back of Kelvin's head as the bus roared away.

Chasing Kelvin

Kofi had no idea where he was going. The bus took a few turns he didn't recognise and, after a short while, he was in a part of London he'd only ever really seen on television.

The skyline stretched off into the distance, lined with a jagged selection of buildings and domes. The bus reached the Thames and Kofi arched his neck to see how far it ran through the city. Bridges punctuated the swirling grey-brown waters which met bright white skies.

Kofi was so caught up in what he was seeing that he

almost missed Kelvin getting off the bus. He sprang to his feet and swung after him, leaping down the stairs and out of the middle doors. The bus chugged away as Kofi spun left and right, just in time to catch Kelvin and the headscarf woman disappearing round a corner.

He followed.

Kelvin led him back towards the river. The streets here were wide and paved with large, creamy-coloured slabs. It was very different to the grimy concrete that Kofi had grown up with on the estate. Kelvin and his partner took a left into some quiet streets, lined with high-posted, wrought-iron fences. There was hardly anyone about, so Kofi had to take care not to get too close.

Eventually, Kelvin reached a huge, light-coloured stone building that looked very old and very grand. The woman opened her arms wide and nudged Kelvin with her elbow. Kelvin rolled his eyes. Then they disappeared inside. Judging from Kelvin's reaction, Kofi decided that the mystery woman must be his mum.

Kofi looked up. The building reminded him of the library on the high street, just bigger. And cleaner. He went in.

It was cavernous, with high ceilings and light flooding in from massive windows far above. A small number of people were milling around and no one seemed to notice either of the children who had just walked in on a weekday morning. Maybe it was a library. Kofi couldn't help but look up as he walked, gazing like a tourist. He caught a glimpse of his reflection in a large pane of glass and momentarily thought Gloria was on the other side of the window. He really did look like his sister. He paused to admire his legs and realised that Kelvin was out of sight.

Up there. Kelvin had disappeared up a winding staircase on to a higher floor of the quiet building. Kofi had lost him. He hooked a thumb into his bra strap and jiggled it into something like a comfortable position, then raced up the staircase, anxious not to lose Kelvin in this giant building after coming all this way.

Kofi rounded the corner at speed straight into a pair of arms carrying a tray of cakes and soft drinks. Everything crashed to the floor, creating a pool of liquid that Kofi instantly slipped in, collapsing to the floor in an ungainly spread of limbs.

'Aargh!'

Kofi looked up at Kelvin's bewildered face. Kelvin looked down at the girl who had just run into him. A group of people sitting at a nearby table looked over to see what all the fuss was about. The woman in the headscarf had just appeared. She looked down at the mess. When she spoke, it was in a broad East London accent, dropping the *H*'s. She nudged Kelvin in the arm.

'Well, help her up, then!'

A Surprise for Kelvin

'Sorry, Kelvin,' said Kofi, scrambling to his feet.

'Oohhh . . .' sang the woman in the headscarf, putting a hand on her hip. 'So you *know* each other, do you? You didn't tell me you had a little *girlfriend*, Kelvin.'

She pinched both of Kelvin's cheeks and waggled his face. Kofi hastily picked up the fallen tray. Kelvin wriggled free.

'So go on then,' the woman continued. 'What's her name, Romeo? *Juliet?*'

She let out a little whoop of laughter at her joke.

Kelvin looked like he was ready for the ground to swallow him up whole.

'*Mum!*'

I knew it, Kofi thought to himself. This was Kelvin's mum. But he never pictured someone like this.

'I-I-I—' Kelvin spluttered.

'*Gloria*,' said Kofi, confidently extending one hand and smoothing down his skirt with the other. 'I'm Gloria. I know Kelvin from s-s –'

He paused. He couldn't say 'school'.

'– sssssomewhere,' he said finally.

'*Ooooh*,' sang the woman, shaking Kofi's hand with a delicate grip. '*Very* mysterious.'

Then to Kelvin: 'Next time you have a secret girlfriend, tell me.'

She laughed wildly. This woman was clearly … *different*, thought Kofi to himself. She turned to face him.

'So sorry, my love. I think he left his manners on the bus. Can't keep hold of anything. Lost his *bag* last week.' She playfully rocked Kelvin's shoulder. 'Let me get us some more cake. You want a lemonade?'

She didn't give Kofi a chance to answer

'I'll get you a lemonade,' she said with a squint and a slow nod. 'When life gives you lemons …' She trailed off, looking into the middle distance so dreamily that both Kelvin and Kofi turned to see what she was looking at. Then she turned back to Kelvin and spoke in a very audible whisper, gesturing towards Kofi: 'So *pretty*.'

And off she went.

The boys watched her go. Then Kofi spun round.

'Kelvin! It's me!' he hissed, grabbing his friend by the shoulders.

Kelvin recoiled, his mouth open in a petrified O.

'It's me: *Kofi*,' said Kofi through his teeth. 'I'm dressed like a girl.'

'Oh,' managed Kelvin. 'W-w-what are you d-doing here?'

'Long story,' said Kofi, hooking arms with Kelvin and leading them to a round coffee table. 'Where is "here" anyway? And how come you ain't at school? And is that your mum? She's ... nice.'

'She's bonkers,' said Kelvin as they sat down, just about managing to answer the last question. 'She used to h-homeschool me. When I was little.'

'So why you here now?' asked Kofi, flicking his hair out from behind his ears with the back of one hand.

'It's Redge,' explained Kelvin. 'He g-got into an argument with my mmmum about something, so she's taken me out of school. For a while.'

'So where are we now?' asked Kofi, looking around.

'Tate Britain,' replied Kelvin. 'My mum loves a museum.'

Tate Britain, thought Kofi to himself. He'd never heard of it before.

'I-I've been loads,' said Kelvin. 'Mum sssays it's important to *"get a bit of culture"*.'

Before Kofi could reply, a huge voice boomed in their direction, making both boys jump.

'COME HERE, AT ONCE.'

Kofi looked up. It was a truly alarming sight. In front of him was a row of three teachers, obviously (Kofi could tell by the scowls on their faces), looking directly at him. The tallest was a white woman in the middle with her hair tied up in a bun, pulling her features up tightly in a sort of grimace. Kofi was immediately reminded of the killer robot in *The Terminator*, a film he once watched with Emmanuel, which had given him nightmares for a week.

'You were told to be at the meeting place FIVE MINUTES AGO.' There was no emotion in the Terminator's voice, just the unmistakable threat of violence. The short one on her left spoke next, in a voice that was as shrill as it was annoying.

'Miss Nicholls will *not* be pleased to hear of *any* St Ursula's student caught *sneaking off* with *boys* on a school *trip*!'

She was one of those stressy ones who put emphasis on every second word. The third teacher just stood there with her little arms folded tight across her massive chest.

Out of the corner of his eye, Kofi could see Kelvin's mum on the return, laughing with a cafe worker who didn't seem so sure.

'Come along. NOW,' instructed the Terminator, beckoning with a bony finger. Behind the teachers were a straggly group of schoolgirls. Kofi looked down at his tie. He was wearing the same uniform.

'Go!' whispered Kelvin, clocking his mum on the approach. Kofi found himself standing up, bewildered. He drifted like a zombie towards the school group, completely lost as to what to do next.

'Join the *others*!' said Miss Shrill, flapping a hand frantically. '*Back* to the *coach*!'

And Kofi was suddenly swept along with a chattering gaggle of girls from St Ursula's, his sister's school. Before he could think what to do, he had gone with the entire group down and towards the exit.

Kelvin's mum arrived at the coffee table with a tray full of food.

'What happened to your girlfriend?' she asked.

The Girls on the Bus
Are Loud Loud Loud

Kofi was bustled on to the coach with a whole group of girls from St Ursula's, perfectly camouflaged by his uniform and disguise. The coach was full of chatter and noise, with Terminator and the other two teachers pointing at heads and ticking off names on a clipboard register. He had no idea what to do next.

Kofi went as far to the back as he could and sank into a corner seat, draping the hair of his wig over his forehead.

'*We* were sitting here?'

It was said like a question but it was really a command. Kofi groaned. Rudegirls.

'Is this St Ursula's?' he asked.

One of the rudegirls pulled a face like plasticine.

'Are you *new*?' she asked in disgust. 'Get up!'

Kofi sighed and rose to his feet, awkwardly shuffling past while rudegirl number one kissed her teeth and cut her eyes.

He edged his way to an empty seat nearer the middle of the coach, next to a small girl with bunches reading a book. He turned towards her as the coach drew away. He was just about to ask if this was St Ursula's again when his attention was caught by a group of girls further down the aisle, crowded round something and talking in whispers. Kofi craned his neck to see what they were huddled over. He recognised it straight away.

'Oh my god, is that—'

He leaned over to take a better look. He was right.

'Paper Jam!'

Kofi couldn't help himself.

'Where did you get this?' he asked excitedly.

'My sister's in Year Ten,' explained one of the girls proudly. 'She got it down the Junction. *All* the Year Tens and Elevens have it,' she added with undisguised superiority. Then she looked curiously at Kofi.

'Are you new?' she asked. 'I haven't seen you before.'

'Just started today,' replied Kofi, reaching for the magazine. 'Ah yes, this one's got "Don't Walk Away" in it!'

He was amazed to see something he had made in the hands of actual people. It gave him a thrill to think that his work was travelling like this.

'I love that song!' gushed a girl nearby. *'Don't, walk, a-waaaaaay, booooooy . . .'*

As soon as she started singing two or three others joined in the chorus. Kofi couldn't help himself and pitched in, pointing out the high notes and shaking his head like he used to do with Kelvin.

'*. . . I'll be, right there – for – yoooooooou!'*

'GIRLS.'

It was the Terminator. Everyone started giggling. Then they carried on singing 'Don't Walk Away', in secretive hushed tones, reading the words together as the bus wound its way back to school.

Trapped

As the bus pulled round through into the school grounds, Kofi realised he should have spent less time singing along to *Paper Jam* and more time formulating some kind of plan. He didn't know what to do and he had no time to figure something out.

The coach's engine juddered to a halt and there was a nanosecond of quiet before everyone got up and everything happened at once. Teachers were bellowing instructions about next period, girls were chattering away, bags were being pulled from overhead and below seats, and in the midst of it all, no one noticed that a boy dressed as his own sister had sneaked his way on a school trip and all the way back to school.

He let himself get swept off the bus with the crowd and contemplated making a run for it, but the coach had driven so far into the school grounds that he couldn't work out where the exit actually was. And even if he did run, getting caught would leave him in more trouble than he could even imagine. Besides, that Terminator looked like she'd be good in a chase.

Before he knew it, Kofi was in a courtyard with hundreds of girls wearing the same tie as him, all bustling off in the same direction.

He tried to fall back, but it was impossible with all the bodies surging forward. Suddenly, he found himself inside, staring down a series of dark corridors lined with rooms that all looked the same. Schools were scary places when you didn't know your way around.

'O-kaaay!' called a teacher's voice over the noise. 'Year Eights, *straight* to the changing rooms we're late for PE!'

Year 8?

PE?

Changing rooms?!

Full-blown panic erupted in Kofi's chest as he realised that the double doors he'd just walked through were taking him into *the girls' changing room*. He gulped. Some of the girls around him were starting to take off their blazers and loosen their ties. Kofi started backing up. If he could j—

He felt himself get yanked hard and pulled through a door to his right that he didn't know was there.

'What, the *hell*, are you *doing* here!'

Gloria's face was a picture of shock. She had him gripped with two fists by the front of his shirt.

Kofi exhaled deeply.

'Gloria!' he gasped. 'You've got to get me out of here!'

Gloria looked round, quickly scanning the area. Then she released her brother and took him by the arm, leading him away from the chaos of Year 8 PE.

'Don't. Say. A. Word,' she hissed as she dragged Kofi, half trotting to keep up, through the labyrinthine corridors of St Ursula's.

A bell rang faintly and Gloria suddenly changed direction.

'It'll be quieter this way,' she whispered.

Up ahead, a young, pale-faced male teacher appeared, striding with all the confidence of a recently promoted assistant head of year. Gloria reacted.

'Quick,' she told Kofi. 'Hold your belly and look at the floor.'

Kofi did as he was told. The teacher came near.

'Girl trouble,' she said with a grimace. 'Miss said we could go to the toilet to change a tampon.'

At the mention of the word *tampon* the young teacher went red in the face and immediately stepped aside to let them pass.

'Works every time,' whispered Gloria. 'Male teachers only.'

In all his life, Kofi had never seen his sister being properly naughty and getting into or out of trouble. Up close, it was a majestic thing to behold.

First, she asked Kofi for his school telephone number. He told her. Then she asked for the full name of his deputy head. He told her that too. After that, she went to the main office and told them that she had been asked to accompany her cousin in Year 8 to the medical room, leaving Kofi at the door. Then she took Kofi round the corner and past the medical room, where she proceeded to scream twice at the top of her lungs, making Kofi jump. After that, she ducked back into the medical room and told the nurse that a bleeding student had just run down the corridor towards the toilet. Up jumped the nurse and went after this mythical student, leaving the medical room empty. Gloria ushered Kofi inside.

'We've got about three minutes,' she said flatly, closing the door behind them.

'Wow, Gloria,' said Kofi, clearly impressed. 'You done this before?'

Gloria didn't answer. She was looking for the telephone. She found it on a little desk near the treatment table. She grabbed it and dialled the number Kofi had told her.

'Hello? Oh yes, hello.'

Kofi's eyes widened. Her impression of Mum was *amazing*.

'Yes, of course. It's Mrs Mensah. *Sonia* Mensah. I'm just returning a call from the school? They asked me ... Yes, he asked me to let him know if my son would be in today. Unfortunately he won't be, I'm afraid ... No, no, absolutely.'

She was in full flow now.

'OK, thanks. Bye.'

She put the phone down.

'Right, go back to the toilet, go in and go to the last cubicle on the left. Lock the door and *start getting changed*,' she explained. Kofi nodded.

'*Go.*'

Kofi went. As he neared the toilet he saw the nurse, flustered, returning. He slipped through the door and found the cubicle, locking it behind him. Getting changed was a bit tricky in the tight space, but he managed to get into his own clothes. The wig was too securely fastened so he was still fiddling with it when he heard a sharp *tap tap tap* on the door. It was Gloria. He let her in.

'Take this,' she instructed, handing over a laminated card attached to a woven cord. It was the kind you were supposed to wear around your neck and the word VISITOR was printed on it in red letters.

'You *have* done this before,' said Kofi as Gloria started unfixing the clips in his hair.

In a few moments, the wig was off. Kofi scratched at his head furiously.

'OK, what n—' he began, but Gloria cut him off with a finger to the lips. A few moments later, a bell rang.

'*Now*,' said Gloria, unlocking the cubicle.

Out they went.

The corridors were already filling up with bodies so it was easy to melt into the crowd and head to the main reception. They arrived at a glass window with one of those sliding panels to speak through. Gloria beamed a dazzling smile.

'Hi, miss!' she said brightly. 'Just returning this visitor's pass. My brother came to drop off my PE kit and got a bit lost.'

She thrust the pass out in front of her.

'Oh, OK,' said the woman behind the glass, sliding the panel open. 'Just through here.'

Kofi was free to go.

He stepped through a door on the right that led out to the visitors' entrance. The sun was shining brightly in clear blue skies.

'Thanks, Gloria,' he said, pulling his rucksack strap over his head. 'I owe you one.'

'You owe me around *twelve*,' she answered. 'Now go *home*.'

'I will!' called Kofi, running off, his bag swinging side to side.

On the Estate

Kofi didn't go home. He went to the minicab office to spend a few of his trick coins on *Street Fighter II*.

He felt himself relaxing at the sound of the game's familiar bleepy electronic music. It had been a busy day. As he jiggled the joystick left and right, selecting his favourite character, he let a parade of thoughts march through his mind.

Round one!

So Kelvin hadn't disappeared after all . . .

Punch – punch – kick.

He was just being homeschooled by his mum . . .

Kick – punch – block.

It was good to see Kelvin, even if it was only briefly . . .

Kick – down – punch.

He hadn't realised how much he'd missed hanging out with him. Kofi didn't really have any other friends . . .

Down – forward – punch: hadouken!

Unless you counted Leroy. But he wasn't always so easy to talk to. He was always so mean about Kelvin too, calling him 'Reloader' because of his stutter. That was bullying. Kofi wanted to say sorry to Kelvin for not sticking up for him about that . . .

Block – jump – kick – land.

He hoped that he would get the chance to.

You lose.

Kofi let the countdown screen go to zero and sighed. He'd better get going before the after-school rush.

*

Back at the estate, Kofi was thinking his thoughts, walking with slow drags of the feet and kicking random bits of litter across the ground. It wasn't even three o'clock yet so the estate was quiet. All the adults were at work and all the kids were at school. But Kofi could still hear the booming bass coming from the top-floor pirate station. It was like a heartbeat for the whole estate.

He turned a corner two blocks away from his block and gasped.

'*Finally.*'

T's deep voice was a match for the pirate radio bass. Kofi froze to the spot as the lanky teenager circled an arm around his shoulders. His two friends appeared out of nowhere, standing on either side of him.

'We need to talk, innit,' said T quietly. Kofi considered wriggling free and making a run for it, but he had a feeling T would catch him, and he didn't want to risk making him angry. He gulped.

'W-what have I done?' he asked nervously.

T looked up at his friends with a slow smile and laughed. It came out in a rasp.

'What have you *done?*' he eventually said to Kofi, with a slow shake of the head. 'Nah, rudeboy, it's what you're going to *do.*'

T's Request

'Wait, you want me to do *what*?'

Kofi had fully heard what T had said, but his disbelief made him ask again. He looked at T, the cigarette smoker, and the heavyset one with the squint, one after the other.

Free goes on the arcade. That was it. That was all. That's what T wanted. He didn't want to hurt Kofi after all. It turned out that he'd seen Kofi at the minicab tournaments and worked out that he must have been somehow scamming free goes on *Street*

Fighter II. T was into arcades in a big way, but it was an expensive habit. He wanted Kofi to let him in on the secret.

'We go Troc, like, every Friday after school, but it's bare expensive, man,' explained T, waving both his hands around as he spoke. 'Troc' was short for Trocadero, a big entertainment complex in the West End, with the biggest selection of arcades in London.

Kofi almost wanted to laugh. Seeing T getting so excited about arcade games suddenly made him a lot less scary. He felt a combination of shock and relief wash over him, and his whole body relaxed. Then the friend with the cigarette piped up.

'Innit!' he squealed. 'I spent up *all* my pocket money *and* all my haircut money on *one* trip.'

He pushed the cigarette that was dangling between his lips fully into his mouth and started chewing. Kofi blinked twice before he realised it was one of those candy sticks that kids used to eat back in primary school. The ones that came in a little fake cigarette packet.

'Want one?' he said, offering the packet to Kofi.

'I thought you wanted to beat me up and take all of my money,' said Kofi, accepting a sweet.

'What money?' asked the one with the squint, stepping forward.

'Doesn't matter,' said Kofi quickly. Then, pointing: 'How come you had Kelvin's bag?'

'Who's Kelvin?' asked the squinter.

'He's the other one,' said T. 'The one who takes the names in that red book.'

'I thought this was him,' said the squinter, squinting even harder at Kofi.

'Put your glasses on, man!' said the sweet smoker.

Squinter proceeded to remove from his pocket the single most nerdy pair of specs Kofi had ever seen and put them on with a series of rapid eye blinks.

'Oh yeah,' he said. 'My bad.'

'The bag?' said T. 'We just found it and knew you knew him. Here.'

He handed the satchel to Kofi.

'Listen,' said Kofi, deciding to take hold of the situation. 'I can get you the free goes. All I need is a bunch of pennies, a bunch of five p's, some ten p's, and some tinfoil.'

T and his friends nodded vigorously.

'*And* . . . some chewing gum,' added Kofi, mysteriously. 'I'll show you.'

He produced a handful of trick coins from the secret lining of his school blazer and the three boys huddled round to see.

Uncle D Finds Out

Kofi wasn't expecting anybody to be in. When he entered the flat and saw Uncle Delroy, they were both momentarily stunned to see each other.

Uncle D was holding a battered envelope that was thick with five- and ten-pound notes. He thrust it towards Kofi.

Kofi could tell straight away from the look on his uncle's face that he knew the money belonged to him.

'Where you get this money from, Kofi?' Delroy asked.

Kofi's mind immediately started racing through a

series of potential lies and stories he could feasibly spin to his uncle, but Delroy wasn't new to the game.

'Don't lie to me now,' he intercepted. 'Just tell me the truth.'

He took a step towards the boy.

'You been *stealing* something? You been *selling* something?'

With each question, Uncle D took a step closer to Kofi, and was now standing directly above him. Kofi panicked. He quickly worked out which version of the truth to tell his uncle.

'I've been running an arcade tournament with my friends!' The words poured out of him.

'What – for money?' said Uncle D. '*Gambling?*'

Kofi honestly hadn't realised that what he'd done was such a shocking crime.

'No! No!' Words were tumbling out of his mouth before he had a chance to check if they were OK. 'It's just a favour I'm doing for some boys from the estate!'

'You runnin' with dem bad boys from the estate now?' said Uncle D, eyes widening. 'You know I'm gonna have to tell your parents, right?' he added with a raised eyebrow, turning to leave the kitchen.

'No!' Kofi reached after him. 'Uncle, please don't,' he pleaded. 'If I get into any more trouble Mum and Dad are going to make me change schools! Please, it was . . . it was just a little tournament – with my friends.'

Uncle D paused. He'd seen his fair share of trouble over the years. I mean, if anyone ever sat down to actually write *The Incredible Misadventures of Delroy Brown*, they'd need a big pen, a lot of paper and a very healthy supply of exclamation marks.

Kofi turned on his best puppy eyes and even considered fluttering his eyelashes. His uncle softened.

'All right, look,' he began. 'I'm not going to tell your parents dem, yeah?'

Kofi wanted to hug him.

'But *you* are.'

Kofi froze.

'And *this*—'

He waved the envelope of money.

'*This* is done. You heard me? *Finished*.'

'Yes, Uncle Delroy,' breathed Kofi.

'I mean it,' warned Uncle D. 'And I don't wanna hear no more about you runnin' with dem boys off the estate,' he continued, shaking a thick gold bracelet further up on to his wrist. 'They might say they're your friends but trust me, you don't want to get all mix up with the wrong crowd.'

Kofi nodded.

'Especially not at your age.'

Kofi nodded.

'And you can decide when you're going to give this money to your parents.'

Kofi gasped. He would never describe himself as sneaky, or even secretive, but he definitely preferred to keep some parts of his life away from each other. Especially if it meant having to actually explain himself to his parents. If any of this was showing on Kofi's face, Uncle D didn't react at all.

'Now come help me get this television working,' said Uncle D.

Kofi nodded.

The Return of the Reloader

The next two weeks were uncharacteristically quiet in the life and times of Kofi Mensah. He stuck to his promise to end the tournaments, so they dried up (much to the disapproval of Leroy, who drifted away from Kofi as soon as there wasn't any money to be made).

For Kofi, school became a lonely place. The report cards kept coming and people would laugh when he clowned about in class, but he spent long and lonely hours standing outside classrooms, sitting in detention, and walking to the bus stop on his own.

He even thought about hanging out with T, the sweet smoker and the squinter (their real names were Edward and Patrick) but they always seemed to be hanging out much later than Kofi was allowed to be.

And then Kelvin came back.

He just appeared one day at school, standing in the playground amidst a raucous swirl of boys in blazers and rucksacks. Kofi couldn't believe his eyes. It was as if Kelvin had never been gone, and he carried the same quiet energy and wore the same oversized blazer as always. Kofi could have hugged him.

'Kelvin!' he exclaimed in the din of the pre-registration rush. 'What are you doing here?'

It was a stupid question, but Kelvin just shrugged. He started to answer before the warning bell interrupted them.

'Tell me at first break,' grinned Kofi. For a brief moment, the two boys smiled full and broad at each other, happy to be together again. They didn't say it, because it didn't need to be said, but this was a warm reunion and confirmation that they really were best friends.

Then Kofi found himself looking down at his shoes, suddenly overcome with a tight feeling that put a knot in his chest. The memory of the time he had left Kelvin and gone off with Leroy came flooding back to him, along with a wave of guilt and shame.

He looked up slowly at his friend, biting his lip, forcing himself to make eye contact. Kofi regretted walking off with Leroy and leaving Kelvin alone like that. He wished he could put it into words. But Kelvin spoke first.

'S'OK,' he said with a half-smile.

Kofi smiled back, wide with relief.

'Thanks, man,' he replied.

It was good to have his friend back.

The Battle

First break couldn't come quick enough. Kofi had a lot to tell Kelvin and there was even more he wanted to know. Missing school was no big deal for Kelvin. He was used to it. He'd been to three different primary schools in total and spent even longer being homeschooled. He was used to going with the flow, and not asking too many questions.

'... so the tournaments are over, which kind of annoyed Leroy, but he's *big* on the Cussing Matches now,' explained Kofi as they walked through a criss-cross of tennis-ball football matches. 'See?'

He pointed to a pulsing crowd behind the refectory. A Cussing Match was in full flow.

As they approached, Kofi could see Marlon Richards in Year 10 energetically bopping up and down, orchestrating the proceedings like an expert ringmaster. In the middle of the crowd, a skinny Year 9 was in the process of being verbally destroyed by Leroy, who was vicious. He pulled absolutely no punches and had developed a nasty skill of targeting the one thing that his opponent felt most insecure about, then not letting go until total humiliation was complete. There was no one in Year 7 or 8 who could compete at this level, but Leroy had an adolescence about him that put him on a level with the olders. He'd even started picking on some of the kids in his own year group. The Cussing Matches were becoming the perfect place for him to basically bully people in public. For the crowd, it was pure bloodsport, and the '*ooohs*' grew in volume and length with every devastating punchline.

Kofi and Kelvin drew near and the crowd erupted into a scatter of limbs and shoulder grabs. Leroy stood proud and cocky in the centre, a cruel smirk printed across his round, smug face. Whatever he'd just said, it was definitely a winner.

'Naaaah!' shouted Marlon over the noise of the

crowd. 'He did it *again. Again!*' He had the voice of a professional radio presenter. 'Is it *really* playtime? Because Leroy's not playing, man!'

Marlon did a little swaying dance move to punctuate his joke.

'Who's next?'

Before a contender could step up to the plate, Leroy had spotted Kofi and Kelvin. He pointed a chubby finger straight at Kelvin, like a laser.

'Yo. The Reloader's back!' he said, with false enthusiasm. 'I heard they tried to kick him out but he kept st-st-starting again.'

The crowd. Blew. Up. Kofi's face fell into an absolute picture of shock. He wasn't expecting this. Before either of them knew it, the crowd had shifted towards them and Kelvin was surrounded. Marlon Richards was hopping from foot to foot.

'Naaaah! Go again, go again!' he bellowed, pushing Leroy twice in the shoulder. 'Taking *liberties* out here!'

'Oi, this boy is a *tramp*,' continued Leroy without missing a beat. 'I was gonna say something about his shoes but they're talking back *already*, cuz.'

The crowd fell apart laughing. Leroy didn't stop.

'Man told me he was Jamaican but truesay it looks like he's from *Poor-tugal*, innit?'

More laughs. Then he flicked a penny at Kelvin that Kelvin had to dodge to avoid getting hit in the face.

'Here. Doing my bit for charity, innit.'

'*Ooooooh*,' went the crowd.

'You need it more than I do, bruv!'

Utter mayhem.

Kofi caught a glance at Kelvin's face. It was crestfallen. Defeated. Kofi had to do something.

'Leave him alone, man.' He stepped up to look Leroy square in the face.

'Shut up, man,' snarled Leroy, squaring up to Kofi. The atmosphere tensed. A fight would not be a good move, and everyone knew it. A few faces were twisted into cruel leers, egging them on. Kelvin's eyes widened with worry for Kofi.

'You shut up!' spat Kofi defiantly. He wasn't going to back down, not for his best friend.

Kelvin took a step forward.

'What do *you* want, you *fool*,' said Leroy through a scowl. He turned his attention to Kelvin. 'Say something back then.'

Leroy was swaying dangerously close to Kelvin's face. Kelvin was chewing his lip. His fists were clenched and he was staring right back at Leroy's snarling face. Kofi had no idea what might happen next. It suddenly fell quiet.

Kelvin opened his mouth.

Kelvin closed his mouth.

Kelvin opened his mouth.

Leroy attacked.

'See!' he said, goading the crowd. 'This kid is so *lame*. He couldn't *make up* his mind if you put his mum's lipstick on his f-f-f-forehead!'

Leroy had brought the energy back to cusses, but it was cruel sport. Marlon Richards was doubled over laughing. Kelvin's mouth closed and he looked at his shoes. The warning bell rang and everyone started to disperse, laughing and reliving the best of Leroy's cusses. A small group of some of the more notorious olders in Year 11 touched fists with Leroy as they passed. Leroy swaggered off with a group of sycophants, shouldering past Kelvin on the way. Even though Kelvin was used to being overlooked and an expert in being ignored, public humiliation stung hard. Kofi didn't know what to say. There was something nasty about the way Leroy was going for Kelvin. He wasn't sure how, but it felt like a line was being crossed. And then something happened.

Very quietly, but very audibly, and with perfect pronunciation, Kelvin spoke.

'Shut up,' he said.

Leroy turned around.

'What did you say?'

A hush fell. Kelvin spoke again.

'I said, *shut up.*'

There was an audible collective intake of breath.

Kofi had never seen Kelvin look like this before. His jaw was clenched and he was looking directly at Leroy with an intense, burning fury. His fists were clenched by his sides. Kofi had no idea what would happen next. The unmistakable menace of a possible fight loomed in the air.

'Say that again, you little re—'

Before Leroy could finish, Kelvin exploded.

'I said – *shut* your *mouth*, you know the crowd thinks that the things that you say really make the air *stink*, my mind's so quick it'll make your eyes blink, and you smell so bad that we think you need *Lynx* . . .'

A stunned silence befell the whole crowd as Kelvin let fly. It was a torrent of insults and observations, attacking Leroy in a crazy verbal assault. And the whole thing was in *rhyme*. He was *rapping*. Fast. And it didn't stop.

'. . . *I can't speak but believe it I can rap it, I take the biscuit while you're eating the whole packet, you try to act tough but you're just a thick dunce, you skip PE cos you never skip lunch, I know you can't count so you better*

*skip maths, but count on this, you could never diss back,
they know it's all facts and I'm hearing them cheer back
but you still can't hear cos you're thicker than earwax...'*

By now the crowd really *was* starting to cheer back.
Kids were leaning in intently, listening to Kelvin's
intricate flow of words and waiting hungrily for each
punchline, while Marlon Richards pulled increasingly
theatrical expressions in response. It was electric.

*'...you talk war, I'm wishing you thought more, and
don't drop litter that's not what the floor's for, you're
rubbish, and I'm not wrong, here's the thing: everybody
knows you belong in the bin...'*

Leroy's face glitched through a series of emotions
that Kofi hadn't seen him do before. He looked like he
might cry. His eye flickered.

Smack.

The punch caught Kelvin right in the side of the
face. He stopped mid-sentence and fell to the ground.
The late bell rang and a swarm of teachers appeared as
the whole crowd dispersed wildly in twenty different
directions. Before Kofi knew what was happening,
Leroy was being led off by two members of the Senior
Leadership Team, shrugging them off and storming
ahead. Kofi stooped down to Kelvin, who was still lying
flat on his back amidst all the scuffling feet.

'Kelvin!' he said breathlessly. 'That was amazing!'
Kelvin squinted one eye shut and smiled weakly.
'Th-thanks,' he said.

Fresh Starts at
St Campions

Kelvin vs Leroy was the talk of the school. For the rest of the day, all anyone heard about was the epic Cussing Match and how Kelvin had transformed it into a one-sided rap battle. By lunchtime, overblown tales of Kelvin's lyrical assassination were ripping through the St Campions playgrounds.

Leroy had been swept away to Redge's office. Fighting was a serious offence at St Campions. He'd probably be suspended and sent home straight away. Meanwhile, Kelvin had become a minor celebrity. At lunchtime, kids were saying hello and shaking him by the shoulder and telling him he had bars. Even some of the olders in Year 11. Kelvin tried to hide it but he was thrilled with the response. School wasn't so bad after all.

Sitting on the bus on the way home, Kofi asked him for the twelfth time how he'd done it.

'I d-don't knnnow,' he explained, again. 'It's just like, I got *really* angry, angrier than I've ever fffffelt b-before. And the words just c-c-came, jjjuust came out.'

'But all those lyrics!' said Kofi, whipping the seat bar with his rucksack strap. 'Did you just make them up on the spot?'

Kelvin nodded.

'All those rhymes? All those words?'

Kelvin nodded.

'Amazing,' said Kofi. 'It's like you got powers, man.'

Then he spent the rest of the bus journey trying to persuade Kelvin to make up lyrics about *him*. But it didn't work because Kelvin wasn't angry enough and, of course, they were good friends.

Kofi was inspired. That same day, as soon as he got home, he found some lined paper in Emmanuel's things and immediately started writing raps of his own. He'd listened to so much music over the past few weeks that it was easy enough to mimic the flows and rhythms of his favourite rappers. Finding the words to fit was tough, but he was galvanised by what he had seen Kelvin do to Leroy in the playground. As he sat at the foldaway table, chewing thoughtfully on a pencil, he was interrupted by a theatrical gasp from Gloria, who had just walked in with her friend Shanice.

'Oh my days – is my brother actually doing *homework*,' she asked incredulously. 'Are you OK?' she added with mock concern.

'Ha. Ha,' said Kofi sarcastically, making a face. 'I'm writing raps actually.' Then he sprang to his feet energetically, ready to test them out on a new audience.

'Oh lord,' said Shanice with a roll of the eyes. 'Here we go ...'

Kofi was undeterred, and his energy was infectious. He started waving his hands as though he was performing to thousands.

'*Yo, put your hands in the air! And wave them like you just don't care! Cos I got that cash and I got them flows, everybody knows, I'm here!*'

Shanice and Gloria started laughing in spite of themselves and Shanice's feet couldn't help but start tapping with the rhythm. Kofi's energy was hard to ignore. He carried on, springing left and right and clutching an imaginary microphone close to his face.

'I'm wavy like ladies' haaaaair! But tough like some grizzly beaaaar! Cos I got those flows and I make that cash and no I don't like to shaaaare!'

The girls doubled over laughing. It was so ridiculous, but it was hilarious too. Kofi was a natural performer.

'Oh my DAYS, man,' managed Shanice, patting her head and wiping her eyes. 'You're an idiot, you know that?'

It was definitely a sign of affection.

'So then, Mr *Cash* and *Flow*,' she continued, falling on to the sofa and taking the remote. 'What you gonna call yourself then?'

Kofi stopped for a second. Then he grinned.

*

That term at school, the effect of what Kelvin had done was seismic. Within weeks, the Cussing Matches were completely transformed. Kids were turning up with scraps of paper, notebooks, even school exercise books, full of lyrics they had written themselves. Suddenly, it wasn't enough just to turn up and cuss an opponent with witty one-liners. Now you had to do it in rhyme. Kofi could barely contain his pride. He was properly happy for Kelvin. He felt like a big brother – someone who had helped Kelvin to come out of his shell. Sometimes, he found himself just grinning at his friend, which would make Kelvin grin back, and then they would fall about laughing.

Kelvin had set a high standard but it was incredible how St Campions rose to the challenge. A whole new generation of St Campions lyricists emerged, trading bars in dazzling displays of verbal wordplay. Not everybody was as good as Kelvin of course, but the battles were always exciting. There was something about the addition of rhyme and rhythm that made the matches extra thrilling.

Another surprise: these rap battles started to attract an entirely different crowd. Kids who previously would never have stepped into the ring were emerging from the shadows. Quiet, nerdy kids who were good with words and fluent with the pen, able to write bars that a lot of the louder kids couldn't. It was a new playing field.

Kofi loved it. Because of *Paper Jam*, he'd become something of an expert in hip-hop and rap. He had carried on listening to Emmanuel's tapes, even after they stopped making the magazine. Alongside Kelvin, he had a new circle of friends, united by a shared love of songs, lyrics, words and music, trading bars on the way to the bus stop. He'd taken to calling himself *the*

CashFlow Kid, which Marlon Richards then shortened to *CashFlow*, and it was starting to stick. Meanwhile, Kelvin was writing more than ever, but he only shared his lyrics with Kofi. And everyone was waiting patiently for him to repeat his legendary performance.

Leroy eventually came back. When he did, he was a far more muted presence than before. His reputation had suffered irreparable damage after the battle with Kelvin, so now he spent most of his time skulking about with a small group of dodgy characters in Year 10. Whenever Kofi and Kelvin passed him, they would look the other way. Apart from the one occasion where Leroy deliberately shoulder-barged Kofi.

It was lunchtime and a group of the Year 7s were in the middle of one of the new and improved battles. Kofi was in a good mood. He had spent the previous night writing his own version of 'Nuthin' but a "G" Thang' by Snoop Doggy Dogg and Dr. Dre – instead of doing his maths homework. The crowd pulsed to four-four rhythm being clapped out by happy hands and stamped on by dancing feet. Kofi couldn't help himself. He jumped in.

'Ah, yeah, it's CashFlow!' started Marlon, hosting with enthusiasm. 'Let's see what he's got!'

Kofi didn't hesitate:

One, two, three and to the four,
Listen to me rapping and start picking up your jaw
Ready to make a difference so pack that up
Because your lyrics are not bad enough
Gimme the microphone first, and watch me pop
like a bubble
I'm like a teacher when I'm spitting cos you know
you're in trouble
And I thought that I should men-tion
You're boring like deten-tion
And here is one last ques-tion
What made you even step to me?
You're a mess to me
And actually,
Your whole life is like a catastrophe
I make you say 'God' like blasphemy
And your shoes look hole-y, naturally
I'm the CashFlow kid, no matching me
I got flows and I make cash you see
Everybody knows I'm a – hey!

It was at that point that Leroy walked past and deliberately barged into Kofi's shoulder, mid-flow.

'Oi, watch it!' is what Kofi said.

'*Shut up,*' is how Leroy replied.

'You shut up, *wasteman*,' is how Kofi ended it.

Then the bell rang for the end of break.

And that was almost the last time they spoke to each other.

Decision Time

It had been weeks since Uncle D had found out about Kofi's secret stash of money, but Kofi still hadn't given it up to his parents. Every time Uncle D passed him in the hallway, he would raise his eyebrows as if to say *Well?*, which was his way of telling Kofi that time was running out. If he didn't say something soon, he knew that his uncle would.

They were in the front room watching *EastEnders*. Kofi was flat on his front, gazing at his Game Boy, Mum and Dad were on the three-seater sofa, and Gloria was curled up on one of the single-seaters, writing something in a notebook. Uncle D was out having a run and Emmanuel was out with 'a friend'. Kofi wasn't sure, because big brothers don't always share this information with their little siblings, but he was almost certain that this 'friend' was actually a *special* 'friend', as in a 'girlfriend'. He was looking forward to teasing him about it later.

Mum tapped her foot and drummed the arm of the sofa nervously, trying to stop herself from looking around: Jeanette was making dinner. She had insisted, and because Mum still hadn't worked out how to say '*no way, are you crazy?*' without sounding offensive, the plan had gone ahead.

On the telly, the East Enders continued to shout at each other in cockney accents.

Suddenly, a plume of steam billowed into the room. Out wobbled Jeanette, precariously balancing four plates on two arms.

'Here we are!' she said breathlessly, leaning dangerously close to the door frame as she turned off the kitchen light switch with her nose. 'Dinner.'

She plonked a plate each in front of each person in the front room, finishing with Mum.

'We didn't have any cream,' she explained, removing

four forks from the back of her jeans pocket. 'So I just used milk.'

Everyone looked down curiously at the plate of food in front of them. Kofi lifted a forkful and let it fall with a splat back on the plate. He looked up at Dad, who was using his fork to push something slowly around his plate. Then he looked at Gloria, who looked at Mum, who looked at her plate, then looked at Jeanette.

'It ... looks lovely,' tried Mum, unconvincingly. Jeanette beamed and bit her bottom lip, nodding twice. It was the internationally recognised signal for *go on, try it then.*

Mum slowly loaded a fork and started to lift it to her mouth. She hesitated. Kofi switched off his Game Boy and sat up to look. The *EastEnders* drumbeat pounded in the background. *Doof, doof-doof, doof do-du-du-doof!* Mum opened her mouth.

Dad's muffled cough rescued her. She turned to face him. He had a fork fully in his mouth with his eyes scrunched up half shut, his face twisted into a grimace. He spoke through a strained chew.

'It's ... it's ...'

Everyone watched.

'It's ... actually really – *nice*,' he said, relaxing his face, unable to mask his surprise.

'Really?' said Mum and Jeanette in unison, both as surprised as each other.

Jeanette pressed her hands together. 'I haven't tasted it,' she said. 'I don't eat cream.'

'Milk,' corrected Kofi, letting another plop fall to his plate.

'*Mmmm*,' said Mum. 'Jeanette,' she continued, pushing her fork through the unidentifiable sloppy mush on her plate. 'This *is* lovely. What is it?'

'Lasagne,' said Jeanette, picking up the remote.

The front door clacked open, followed by the sound of Emmanuel putting his keys in the key bowl.

'So how was your *date*?' called Mum, finishing her forkful and nudging Dad with her elbow.

'Did you kiss her?' called Kofi, sitting up.

'Kofi!' hissed Dad.

Emmanuel entered the room.

'So *did* you kiss her?' asked Mum with a smile.

'Sonia!' said Dad.

'Good girls don't kiss on the first date,' mumbled Gloria, not looking up.

'How would you know?' said Dad, alarmed.

Kofi opened his mouth to say something but was interrupted by the sound of Uncle Delroy clattering into the hallway, back from his run. Suddenly remembering what he hadn't done, Kofi jumped to his feet and dashed into the hallway.

'Have you done it yet?' said Uncle D, catching his breath after sprinting up five flights of stairs.

Kofi spoke like a cornered wasp.

'Well, I was going to, Uncle, I swear, but then, but then, but then only Mum was in and I wanted to tell them both so I thought maybe I should pretend that I found it after—'

Uncle D raised a hand to interrupt.

'You're one of them people that's so clever you can't do simple no more. Come.'

He led Kofi back into the living room.

'Question number *five*,' Gloria was in the middle of saying. 'How many *hairstyles* has she had in the last six mont—'

'Yo,' Delroy interrupted. Everyone turned to look.

'Kofi got something to say.'

All eyes turned to Kofi. He swallowed.

'Jeanette's lasagne is *fantastic*—'

Uncle D shot him a look that very quickly shut him up. Jeanette put two thumbs in the air and mouthed, 'Thanks.'

'The *truth*,' said Uncle D to his nephew. '*All* of it.'

Doing the Right Thing

Kofi explained everything to his parents. The tournaments, the money, the coins, everything. Well, everything except the magazines, which no one at home knew about yet. Mum and Dad listened carefully until he had finished. After a pause, Mum slowly unfolded her arms.

'Kofi,' she began. 'I'm proud of you. We both are.'

Dad nodded.

'But you've got a streak in you that just keeps getting you in trouble. Just like my brother did when he was little.'

Dad leaned forward tenderly.

'We're worried, Kofi,' he said softly. 'About what you might get yourself into.'

Kofi looked at the floor. Mum spoke next, her voice firmer than it was before.

'So you're going to take *all* that money you've made, say sorry, and give it back to the minicab office. OK?'

Kofi knew that wasn't even a question.

*

It was Mum's idea for Uncle Delroy to go with Kofi to make his apology and hand over the money. She knew how much her son looked up to her brother, and it was Uncle D who had found out about the money in the first place.

Meanwhile, it was Dad's idea for Emmanuel to go with him. Dad had old-fashioned ideas about the eldest son taking on extra responsibility, and thought it would be good for Emmanuel to help Kofi make amends. On this occasion, Mum and Dad put their ideas into action before they told each other. This is how Kofi ended up going to the minicab office with his uncle and his big brother at the same time.

'Maybe it'll be closed and we'll have to turn round

and go home,' said Kofi hopefully. He'd never made this much money before and wasn't in a hurry to hand it over to a total stranger.

It was Friday evening. Kofi hadn't quite forgiven his uncle for making him tell the truth to his whole family, but he was unconsciously mimicking his swaggering bop.

'Maybe they'll think we're undercover police officers and lock us in the basement for trying to trick them,' tried Kofi. He was getting desperate now.

'Or we could just spend it all on a takeaway?' he said, looking up at Emmanuel and Uncle D in turn.

'Kofi,' said Emmanuel. 'I promised Dad we'd give the money back and say *sorry*. So that's what we're going to do.'

Uncle D nodded wisely.

Kofi sighed. On any other occasion he would have loved being out on a Friday night. The streets felt more alive, more vibrant somehow, lit up with lights and noise and the bustle of everyone starting their weekends. Emmanuel was taking his job very seriously but also kept looking at his watch. He had plans to go out afterwards and didn't want to be late.

A car sped past, blaring out bass-heavy music at a volume loud enough to drown out the engine. Uncle D looked over and raised a fist to say hello. The driver leaned on an elbow out of the side window, raising an arm in response. Uncle D was one of those people who seemed to know everyone, and Friday night was his natural habitat.

'Who was that?' asked Kofi, forgetting that he was supposed to be annoyed.

'Ah, just a friend I used to do a little music ting with back in the day,' said Uncle D wistfully. 'We used to hook up with some boys at a studio down south. Made a few little songs, put out a few little white labels, couple dubplates and that . . .'

A warm smile filled his face as the memories filtered through.

'I was never too hot on the buttons but I killed it on the mic, *trust*.'

'You were an MC?' Emmanuel was impressed.

'Of course!' said Uncle D, somewhere between a scowl and a grin. Then he broke out into a volley of lyrics, growled at a rapid double-time tempo. It was a bit like the ragga artists that Gloria and Shanice liked to listen to, but without the thick Jamaican accent. Kofi tried to keep up but had no idea what he'd just said.

'I didn't know you could *rap*,' he said.

Uncle D tapped the side of his nose with one gold-ringed finger. Kofi wondered what else he didn't know about his uncle. 'They called me *Dreaddy D.*' He laughed with nostalgia. Kofi tugged his brother's sleeve.

'Hey, if you were an MC they could call you *Lanky Emmanuel,*' he said.

Emmanuel made a face.

'Or *Manny Beanpole,*' continued Kofi. 'Or the *Skyscraper* … or … *Stoop Doggy Dogg,* or *Big Lanky Eedyiat Boy*—'

Laughing, he ducked to avoid the clap on the back of the head coming from Emmanuel's direction.

They arrived at the minicab office. It was a small concrete building kind of embedded between a proper shop and a thin alley. There was an open space, and a single door that led to the main office. During the day, the door was always locked. Come to think of it, Kofi couldn't remember ever seeing it open. The arcade machines stood in a dusty row. Kofi vaguely wondered who, if anyone, emptied them for coins and the shock they would receive from getting all of his *sandwiches* and *cover-ups.*

Now it was evening, the office door was open, spilling yellow light into the darkening street. A few drivers sat around reading newspapers and smoking cigarettes, all crumpled leather jackets and bad haircuts. Uncle D led the way through, followed by Kofi, with Emmanuel at the back.

'Where to?'

The man who spoke was sat in an ancient swivel chair that looked like it was screaming for mercy under his weight. He had small eyes and short spiky hair. He was the manager. He reminded Kofi of the gerbil they used to have in his Year 5 class. When it was Kofi's turn to bring it home, Dad pretended not to be scared, but flinched every time it moved in its cage. Uncle D spoke next.

'My nephew has a confession to make,' he said, cryptically. He was naturally dramatic.

The gerbil man looked quizzically at Uncle D, then at Kofi, then at Emmanuel, then back at Uncle D.

'You what?'

His eyes disappeared into a squint. Emmanuel gave Kofi a gentle nudge.

'Tell him,' he said with a nod. Even though Kofi had practised what he was going to say back at the flat (Emmanuel had forced him to), he was reluctant to do it now. He was way more used to talking himself *out* of trouble than admitting he'd done something wrong. He took a deep breath.

'Um. I've been putting fake coins into your arcade machines and running tournaments for money.'

The drivers were starting to listen in. Kofi carried on.

'And I'm here to give you back the money I made.'

Silence.

'And to say sorry,' added Kofi. All the drivers were listening now.

'Sorry,' he said, sheepishly. Emmanuel removed the envelope from his jacket pocket and handed it to his brother, who extended it slowly forward.

The drivers all looked at each other. Kofi looked at the gerbil-man manager. The manager looked back at Kofi. Kofi shook the envelope slightly. The manager leaned back in his chair, puffed out his little cheeks and folded his arms.

'You what?' he repeated.

An Unlucky Encounter

'I still can't believe he let you keep it.'

Emmanuel was shaking his head and holding his temples with the finger and thumb of the same hand. They had left the minicab office and were walking back down the high street, back towards the estate.

'He said I was like his auntie Paneer,' beamed Kofi, proudly.

'He said you were like an *entrepreneur*, Kofi,' corrected Emmanuel.

Kofi didn't know what that meant.

'Yep,' smiled Uncle D, shaking his head. 'You're a natural-born businessman.' He waved across the street at a small group of men leaving the barbershop. 'A *lucky* one too.'

He flashed a mischievous smile.

'Let's celebrate. Chicken and chips. On me.'

Kofi punched the air with joy.

'Can I get ribs?' he asked his uncle.

'Yeah, man,' replied Uncle D. 'Manny?'

Emmanuel looked at his watch. 'Sorry, Uncle,' he said. 'I need to go. I'm running late already.'

'Hot date?' asked Kofi slyly. '*Manny and his girlfriend, sitting in a tree . . .*'

'I'll get this little millionaire home,' said Uncle D, interrupting Kofi's teasing. 'We'll see what your parents dem want to do with the money. Come.'

He touched fists with Emmanuel, who went off at a jog towards the bus stop. Kofi and Uncle D headed off to Chick King Chicken, Kofi bopping up and down like a five-year-old. He was in a good mood, and Chick King always threw extra chips in the bag when they put the box in. And there was the free ketchup. Heaven.

Five minutes later, the pair were emerging from the chicken shop with a fat bag of chicken, chips and ribs, and a thin white carrier bag containing two Lilts and a bunch of serviettes. A couple of streets later, Uncle D was right in the middle of an anecdote about him and Mum when he suddenly stopped. He thrust a hand into his jeans pocket and withdrew a handful of coins. He scowled.

'Ey, dem man there just gave me change for a ten and I paid with a twenty!' He handed a bag to Kofi. 'One second, little man, stay here.'

And he left.

The streets weren't empty, but they weren't busy either. Kofi had little choice but to stand and wait until his uncle came back with the right change. He was only eleven, but he'd already learned the lesson that black boys learn fast on the streets of London: that when you're out on your own, you keep moving. Because if you stop, you might get noticed, and if you get noticed, you might be a target. And if you're a target, you might become a victim. And no one wants to be a victim.

'Coin*boy* . . .'

The voice came in a slow drawl through the cool night air. Kofi hadn't seen him coming. It was Leroy. And he wasn't alone.

Kofi noticed two of the others from Year 10 or 11 from St Campions, but like everyone else, they looked older in their own clothes.

'Who's this?' said one of them in a flat monotone. Kofi knew how to respond in this kind of scenario: say nothing, nod at most, and put bass in your voice if need be. He made a conscious effort to keep his eyes at a cool half closure.

'Kofi,' he said, trying to keep his voice low and flat.

'He wasn't talking to you, blud,' snapped Leroy. The atmosphere switched. Something had already gone wrong. Kofi looked in the direction his uncle had just gone. He started to walk.

'Ey, where you going, rudeboy?' said Leroy, stepping in Kofi's way. 'Where you running to, *CashFlow*? Ain't you going to tell me to shut up? *Wasteman*.'

Kofi tried to look away, but Leroy kept moving his head around to hold his gaze. He suddenly felt very alone.

'Wha's this?' said Leroy, suddenly snatching at the bag of food Kofi was carrying. 'You brung me something to eat?'

One of the other boys laughed.

Kofi moved the bag out of Leroy's reach, and Leroy snatched for it again. Then one of Leroy's friends who had sidled round to Kofi's side grabbed it from his hand.

'Hey!' protested Kofi, but it was too late. The bag was being ripped open.

Kofi lunged forward, but a strong block sent him scudding backwards. A few pedestrians started to cast wary glances.

'Give it!' squealed Kofi, the treble in his voice betraying him.

'*Give it*,' mocked Leroy, laughing deep and low. 'You *chief*.'

'*Yo.*'

Uncle D's voice came loud and crisp from about twenty metres up the street. He sprinted in long, powerful strides towards his nephew and the others.

'Wha'you doing?' he said, looking each boy full in the face.

Leroy was momentarily stunned by the appearance of this dreadlocked saviour, and his two friends took a physical step back. Kofi's heart fluttered with relief. But he didn't want to go into helpless mode just like that. Despite everything that had gone on between them, there was a code to observe.

'Oh, Uncle, they're just some ... some friends from school.'

Uncle D wasn't having any of it.

'These dem boys from the estate been troubling you?'

'Ay, we don't know this yute,' said one of the older boys.

Leroy recovered his cool.

'You runnin' to your uncle now?' he laughed. 'You *idiot.*'

'Watch your mouth, boy,' warned Uncle D, pointing a gold-ringed finger into Leroy's face.

The next bit happened fast.

Leroy instinctively swatted at Uncle Delroy's arm, and batted it out of his face. As he followed through, his arm jolted Kofi's shoulder. Kofi pushed back, prompting friend number one to say, 'Don't get rude,' and fully push Kofi with a two-handed shove to the chest. This made Kofi stumble backwards towards the kerb, where he slipped into the road. A car screeched to a halt to avoid hitting him.

The car was a police car.

Running Out

The front doors of the police car flew open like insect wings and out jumped two police officers. One of them was a wiry woman with a frowny scowl where her eyes, nose and mouth should have been. The other was an open-faced man with a slightly sweaty sheen, who reminded Kofi a bit of Mr Redge. It was hard to work out which of the two was more exasperated because they both slammed their doors shut as they approached the scene.

'Oi!' called the male officer. 'You tryna get yourself killed?'

Kofi scrambled back to the pavement. The male officer planted himself directly in front of Uncle D while his partner raked her eyes across the faces of Leroy and his friends.

Kofi watched with a new combination of fear and dread as his uncle leaned his head backwards and looked away. There was something going on here that his uncle knew well, but he had never seen before, and it felt ... dangerous.

'What you up to, fellas?' said the male officer in a too-loud voice, addressing everyone but keeping his eyes locked with Uncle D.

'Get against that wall,' instructed the female officer. 'All of you.'

The boys started to protest.

'NOW,' she added, reaching for the little radio at her lapel.

A small crowd of onlookers was starting to gather across the street. Kofi looked up helplessly at his uncle, but Delroy was still in that position of forced submission, pinned to the spot, unable to move. Kofi could see his uncle's chest pulsing. He was either very scared, or very angry. The bag of chicken and chips lay slumped on the ground.

'... yeah, five I-C-three males ... we almost ran into one ... appeared to be fighting in public on the corner of ...'

The female officer was radioing in. Kofi saw Uncle D's eyes flare.

'Fighting? They're just kids, man—'

'No one said *talk*,' snapped the male officer. 'Get names,' he instructed his partner.

'We didn't do nothing!' called out one of Leroy's friends, stepping forward in complaint. His movement was met with a firm stride and blocking arm from the female officer, putting a hand hard on his shoulder.

'Don't touch me!' called the youth, shrugging violently. The female officer was jolted slightly. Her partner wheeled around and instantly had the boy against the wall in an expertly administered restraining manoeuvre.

'Behave!' he snarled.

Uncle Delroy couldn't.

'He's just a yute, man!' he said, reaching a thick arm out and pulling the officer back by the shoulder.

The next moment was a blur. Both officers had Uncle D pinned to the ground, struggling to hold him still as he writhed. Kofi's mouth was a perfect O as he watched helplessly. The female officer was radioing in again, calling for backup. The sound of a siren started to cut through the air.

Then an elbow was thrown.

Kofi couldn't tell exactly when it happened, but he knew it came from his uncle.

'*Requesting assistance . . .*' The envelope of money was pulled out of Uncle D's pocket. The flash of silver from swiftly produced handcuffs. A flurry of movement. '*Assailant is in possession of a large quantity of cash.*' What looked like a bruise had appeared on one of the officers' faces.

'Calling for BACKUP, *NOW,*' Kofi heard someone shout. It sounded far away. His head swam.

And then he ran.

The Last Coin

Kofi was running quicker than he'd ever run before, but his thoughts were racing even faster. The streets were a blur as he sprinted away, feet barely touching the ground.

He was panicking. He'd run away from the police. His uncle was getting arrested. He couldn't go home, not now. What would he say to his parents? How could he explain this? He couldn't and he knew it.

Still running, Kofi felt a sickening sensation in the pit of his stomach but didn't slow down. A siren wailed in the near distance and he darted left. This was more trouble than he had ever been in before. His uncle had just hit a police officer.

Kofi paused for breath and leaned his back against a wall, letting his head fall backwards against the rough bricks. His lungs were burning but he didn't care. Then he let his head fall forward, hands on his knees. He tried to think but his thoughts were all a jumble. He thought about what might be happening to Uncle Delroy and shuddered. He'd hit a police officer.

You can't hit a police officer.

You get arrested for that.

You go to prison for that.

Kofi closed his eyes.

The trundle of a bus stopping at traffic lights shook him alert. It was an open-backed one that was headed for the Junction. Emmanuel was at the Junction. Emmanuel would know what to do. With a confusion of thoughts muddling through his head, Kofi ran towards the bus and hopped on the platform as it pulled away.

*

The bus ride gave Kofi a bit of time to think. He hopped off before the conductor had a chance to ask him for a fare and started on his walk towards the Junction, keeping his eyes peeled for any stray police in the vicinity. As far as Kofi knew, they carried radios and might be out looking for him right now.

He knew he had to call home. Unless he wanted to go on the run forever, that was the best thing to do.

A phone booth stood a few metres ahead. Kofi stepped in. He rummaged in his pockets and produced a sweet wrapper, some lint and a single twenty-pence piece. It was probably one of Emmanuel's.

He lifted the receiver and raised the coin to the coin slot. He realised he was shaking and could feel his heart beating in his chest. He didn't know what he was going to say, and didn't want to imagine what his parents might say to him.

The coin dropped in with a hollow clatter. He started to dial.

Engaged

'Innit doe!'

Gloria was pressed up against the door of her little box room. She had stretched the phone handset as far as it could go, until it was just about able to reach into her room. It meant that she had to sit on the floor, but it was better than having her weekly debrief with Shanice in the hallway.

As usual, Shanice was doing most of the talking. Mum and Dad were in the front room. Uncle D had told his sister that he'd treat Kofi to a meal out after handing back the money, so they were relaxing in an unusually quiet flat.

'You on the phone, Glo?' called a voice from the front room.

'One sec, Shanice,' said Gloria, before covering the mouthpiece with one hand. 'ALMOST FINISHED, DAD, AND FOR YOUR INFORMATION, SHE CALLED ME.'

In the front room, Dad looked at Mum.

'I didn't even say anything...'

Into the Night

Kofi rested his head on the glass of the phone box. The line was engaged. If it was Gloria, it might be all night. He sighed. He didn't have any more money anyway. And he didn't have anybody else to call.

And then he remembered.

There was a way of getting free calls on public telephones. All you had to do was pick up the receiver and press the little buttons like Morse code, once for 1, twice for 2 and so on. He'd never tried it, but some kids at school had sworn it worked. He had nothing else to lose.

And then he remembered something else.

He *did* have somebody else to call. Apart from his school telephone number, and the Saturday morning phone-in number for *Live & Kicking*, it was the only other telephone number that he knew off by heart. Kelvin.

Kofi lifted the receiver and carefully started tapping the contact buttons, making sure to leave a gap between each number. It took a short while. He looked around as a few cars sped along the main road. It was properly dark now.

Nothing.

And then...

... something.

A tone, not quite a dialling tone, but something close.

'Kelvin?' Kofi whispered. Was anyone on the other end? He tried again:

'Kelvin? *Hello?* Anybody there?'

Nothing.

His grip loosened around the receiver.

'I know you can't hear me,' he said softly. '... I'm just ... I'm just so scared. I'm *scared*. I've ... I've done something so stupid and I don't know how to fix it. I've been so stupid. This keeps happening and I know I have to change. You can't run away from the police. All this stuff I've done, the magazines, the money, the coins, it's not worth it – it's never worth it . . .'

He was talking to himself. He was tired and scared and angry at himself. And suddenly it was all coming out. How he was so stupid. How he kept on getting into trouble and now the police had his uncle and it was all for nothing. How he had run away from the police and made it worse, all for some money that he couldn't keep anyway. How he was going to be kicked out of school and he hadn't made it through one year. How badly he had let his parents down and he couldn't even tell them.

The words poured out. It was like a tap had been opened up on all of Kofi's thoughts and fears. He couldn't stop himself.

When he had finally finished talking, he kicked the phone booth in frustration. It was time to end this. He had to go find his brother. He leaned out of the booth and the wind whipped cruelly around his shoulders as he tripped into the night.

Kofi on the Run

The next twenty-five minutes were the longest twenty-five minutes of Kofi's life so far.

The Junction was as busy as he expected it to be and nearly impossible to find one person in. Kofi felt small, lost and alone. He was drifting in circles from place to place, hoping to just stumble across his brother, despite having no game plan for where to look. There was growing dread in the pit of his stomach over what might be going on at home. The whole thing felt like one of those bad dreams where you have to get somewhere or reach something, but you can never quite make it.

After his third desperate circuit of the food court, he was about to give up all hope, when an unexpected voice interrupted his despair.

'Kofi?'

He looked up.

'Emmanuel!'

His brother was clearly surprised.

'What are you doing here?'

A crowd had gathered outside the Cineplex, getting ready to go in. With Emmanuel having turned up out of nowhere like that, Kofi felt a rush of relief like he had never felt before.

'Kofi?'

It wasn't his brother speaking. Kofi's head swivelled in the direction the voice had come from.

'Kofi Mensah?'

Kofi's eyes grew wide with fear. There were four very important things Kofi didn't know about the police, that he was just about to find out:

They had arrested Uncle Delroy for assaulting a police officer.

They really hated it when people ran away from them.

They had radios.

They knew Kofi had gone to the Junction.

A young police officer stood at the cinema entrance beside an overweight security guard. He was pointing at Kofi.

'Kofi?' said Emmanuel in disbelief. 'What? What's going on?'

The police officer strode forward, radioing something inaudible into his radio unit. He looked determined.

'Do *not* run this time,' he said firmly.

Emmanuel was alarmed. Kofi froze.

'Kofi, what did you *do?*' he said, panicked. The police officer instantly threw a gaze at him.

'Do you know this boy?'

The officer's eyes narrowed. There was hardly any noise for him to talk over. He repeated the question.

'Do you know this boy?'

Emmanuel instinctively raised both hands.

'He's my brother,' he said, flatly.

Kofi looked from Emmanuel to the police officer and back to Emmanuel. The officer broke the silence.

'Both of you are coming with me.'

It wasn't a request.

Kofi tried to catch his brother's eye but he was staring dead ahead, not looking at anyone.

'Come on, Kofi,' he said.

Rainfall

The drive back was a quiet one. The two brothers sat in the back seat of the police car, letting the sounds of the night take the place of conversation.

Kofi was exhausted. His head was resting against the window, rain pattering on the glass. He wanted to speak to his brother, to explain what had happened, to ask for reassurance that everything would be OK, but he didn't know how to start.

There was something else too. He'd known his brother long enough to know that he was upset. Not just annoyed, like when Kofi called him names or borrowed his stuff, but really deep down upset, and troubled. Kofi glanced at his brother, who looked just like he did when he was ashamed. Ashamed and humiliated. Emmanuel was the only black face in his entire friendship group at college, and he had once told Kofi about the weight of having to fit in, when he stood out. Kofi knew his brother well enough to know that he didn't want to be that black boy who got into trouble. He didn't want to be that stereotype. And then the police turned up.

Kofi didn't know any of this, but he felt it. And he was sorry. He looked over at his brother again, but his brother was looking away.

The rain continued to fall.

*

The police station was all hard surfaces and harsh glare. Kofi and Emmanuel were not under arrest, but they weren't free to go. They were sitting on a bench, waiting for a responsible adult to come and collect them. Their parents were on their way.

Kofi wanted to talk to his brother but he still didn't know what to say, so they sat in silence.

He watched as a string of people in various states of

distress were paraded in front of the counter. Some were drunk. Some shouting abuse. Some were drunk and shouting abuse. Emmanuel's eyes were closed.

Kofi had no idea what time it was when Mum and Dad came rushing in. Before he knew what was happening he was bundled up in his mother's arms and he found himself sobbing uncontrollably. Dad had Emmanuel's head cupped in his hands, pressing foreheads together. Mum turned to the desk.

'So you couldn't bring them home?'

Her voice was edged with steel. The officer behind the desk drew a deep breath, as if to begin a weary explanation, but Mum raised a hand to stop her.

'Sonia?'

Kofi turned. It was Uncle Delroy, on the other side of the desk in a walkway that led deeper into the station. All of his gold jewellery was gone and he was in handcuffs, flanked by two police officers escorting him to a cell. There was a graze along his cheek from where he had been held against the pavement. Mum was not sympathetic.

'How you get my boy in this kind of trouble, Delroy?' she said, her voice loud, and trembling slightly. Dad gently rested a hand on her shoulder. She shook it off and pointed in her brother's face. He tried to start an explanation.

'No, Delroy!' She shook a finger at him. '*No*. You've been doing this your *whole life*. And what's changed? How can I trust you if I can't even *trust* you?'

'Madam, please—' the officer interrupted. Kofi's mind was spinning. He'd never seen Mum angry like this before. And he knew it wasn't Uncle Delroy's fault. He'd been trying to help. Kofi had to say something.

'Mum, I—'

'*Not now, Kofi.*'

Her voice was iron. Kofi shut up.

'Come on, Sonia,' whispered Dad softly. 'Let's go.'

Four weeks later . . .

A Star Is Born

'Kofi?'

'Yes, sir?'

'A quick word?'

It was the end of double English. Mr Downfield wanted to have a chat with Kofi about his work, before first break.

'Great work today,' he said enthusiastically. 'I was hoping we could share it with your form tutor? And maybe you could show it off at celebration assembly? If you didn't mind?'

The way he spoke made everything into a question. Kofi was taken aback. He still wasn't used to all this positive feedback.

'Do I have to?' said Kofi.

'No.' Mr Downfield shrugged. 'But if you don't, then I will.'

They weren't exactly friends, but Mr Downfield could be quite funny when he wanted to.

'See you at Rap Club,' he added with a thumbs up.

School was a bit different since that night with the police. There had been a big meeting between Mum, Dad and Mr Redge, where lots of very serious things were said about Kofi having to find another school if these kinds of things – like getting into trouble in and out of school – were going to keep happening. Kofi thought his parents would be angry, but they were mainly quiet. After that they had lots of Big Talks with him about how he felt, what he'd done and what he wanted to do, with lots of hugs and lots of tears. He wasn't allowed to go to school for three days.

Kofi made a solemn promise to never let his parents down, ever again.

But, if we're being completely honest, the main reason Kofi decided to turn over a new leaf was because of what had happened to Uncle Delroy. The scuffle with the police that night had eventually turned into an arrest, which then turned into a night in a cell, which turned into a court date, which turned into a prosecution, which turned into a caution. What that meant was that Uncle Delroy was given a very strict warning to stay out of trouble. And because Kofi felt responsible for everything leading up to the scuffle in the first place, he had decided the whole thing was his fault.

It wasn't long after the arrest that Uncle Delroy and Jeanette were able to move out of the flat into a place of their own. Uncle Delroy had found work that was outside London somewhere. It wasn't a million miles away, but it meant Kofi wouldn't be seeing his uncle nearly as much as he had got used to. When it was time to leave, everyone gave everyone a big hug. Kofi had struggled to know what to say to Uncle Delroy, but his uncle promised he would come back to see everyone soon, so it wasn't a sad departure.

Almost putting your favourite uncle in prison is a heavy burden for any eleven-year-old to bear, and Kofi was determined to put things right. Once a week, every week, Kofi would sit at the foldaway table beneath Gloria's lamp and write a letter to Uncle Delroy, telling him about everything that was happening at home. He wrote slowly and carefully, making sure every word could be read perfectly.

At school, the Cussing Matches were well and truly over. The rap battles that had replaced them had evolved too. They were now *cyphers*, a word Kelvin had introduced to St Campions that had caught like a lit match. A *cypher* was a circle where absolutely anyone was invited to rap. Not in competition, but together. Cyphers were uplifting and energetic, full of encouragement and joy and people rapping as one. All the insults and battling was over. Now it was all about lyrics and fun.

Lunchtime came around quicker than usual.

'All right all right *all right*! Who's up *first?*'

Marlon Richards was doing a little snaky body-popping movement with his arms and sliding around on his heels and toes at the same time. It was the start of lunchtime on a bright Thursday afternoon and the crowd was getting warmed up.

A gathering group of St Campions' blazers had formed an excited crowd in the corner of the big playground. There were faces from all the year groups – youngers too – all getting ready for the big cypher. Some were busy repeating lyrics to themselves silently, while others were shuffling through scraps of paper with line upon line of brand-new rhymes scribbled on.

As usual, Kofi was just taking it all in. This was his favourite time of the day, by far. Back in Year 6, he had once taken part in a big school play that had run for two nights in a row. The atmosphere at the start of the cyphers reminded him of opening night. It was electric, crackling with possibility and excitement. The old Cussing Matches had been exciting, but this was different. There was no threat now that something *cruel* was about to happen, just the promise that something *cool* was about to happen, which was much, much better.

'You gonna rap today?'

Kofi aimed his question at Kelvin, who stood quietly next to him. Everyone knew that Kelvin could rap, but he had only stepped up to the front twice since that amazing freestyle against Leroy. He looked at Kofi, shrugged and half-smiled in response.

'Come on, man,' coaxed Kofi. 'You were wicked last time!'

It was true. Kofi had somehow forced Kelvin to do one of his latest verses a few days ago. Marlon had made him start from the beginning twice because it was so good. He kept saying '*The Reloader's back!*' but in a good way. His confidence was going up.

Before Kofi could fully talk Kelvin into stepping into

the cypher again, a tiny Year 8 with picky hair and thin metal glasses nudged his way past them, taking up his place right in front of Marlon Richards.

'Oooh!' exclaimed the compère in perfect mock surprise. 'We have a newcomer!'

The boy with the picky hair wiped his nose with the back of his hand. His name was Michael Ibe, but everyone in his year called him 'Ibby'. He wasn't what you would call a popular kid, but in the cyphers, everyone was given a chance. Those were the rules.

'Let's see what he's got!' blared Marlon. A small group of Year 10s started stamping out a rhythm with their feet. A few others started clapping along and Marlon pursed his lips, saying 'Go, go, go' on every two count.

Ibby went.

'Like a cat cos I always land right on my feet, when the rhythm's really banging I'm right on the beat, I'm a street light cos I'm so bright in the street, and I write right when it's rhyme time for the week ...'

The crowd lit up, all wide eyes and fists held against mouths in shock. There was a flurry of *oohs* and *aahs*, but Marlon waved his hands to keep everyone quiet enough to keep on listening.

'... I'm a geek, can't you tell by the specs on my face? When it comes to the rhymes I'm the best in the place, no

lies, all facts, no pointless debate, and I'll tell you the same when we meet face to face—'

The boys playing football had stopped to come nearer and listen in now. It was electric. Ibby was in full flow.

'. . . *You can hear this, feel this, get this real, this stuff is simply rid-i-cule-lis, nuts it's crazy, I'm so shady. Hi then bye cos I'm so wavy. Play me, loud, when you're hearing my song, no slacking is allowed when I'm coming this strong, no beat is ever ever ever ever too long, and I know that you lot just love it so I'll just carry on!*'

The crowd erupted, with a number of boys running off in scattered directions and coming back to jump on each other. Little Ibby stood in the middle of it all with a dazed smile on his face, Marlon Richards side-hugging him and shaking his shoulder violently. By popular demand, Ibby started his verse again, from the top. This time, the whole crowd was joining in with the last word of every punchline.

'This is so sick,' said Kofi, grinning from ear to ear.

Getting On

It was Sunday afternoon and the flat was quiet. Kofi was hanging backwards off the edge of the sofa, playing his Game Boy upside down, the TV droning on in the background. Gloria was in her box room, Dad was at work and Mum was on her way back. The door rattled on the chain and Kofi heard it clatter open and shut.

Emmanuel walked into the front room, his long arms dropping a bag gently by the door. Kofi barely glanced up.

Emmanuel paused, looking around the room.

'You watching this?' he asked Kofi.

Kofi clicked furiously on his Game Boy. 'Mm-mm,' he said through closed lips. That meant no.

Emmanuel strode over to the set and pushed the 'off' button.

'Hey,' protested Kofi, swinging on to his feet. 'I was watching that.'

'Kofi,' began Emmanuel, sitting slowly on the edge of the sofa. 'You all right?'

Kofi paused slightly before turning back to the falling blocks of *Tetris*. Emmanuel gently took the Game Boy out of his hands.

'You OK?' repeated Emmanuel. He was looking directly into Kofi's eyes and it made the smaller boy want to look away. Emmanuel continued.

'Listen, I've been hearing you. At night. You're having bad dreams.'

Kofi looked down. It was true. He had been having bad dreams. He'd woken up at night a few times in a mild panic and his brother must have noticed. Emmanuel let his head lean slightly to one side and carried on.

'It's not your fault, OK?' There was an awkward silence. 'What happened with Uncle Delroy – don't blame yourself. I'm serious.'

Kofi went to get his Game Boy but Emmanuel intercepted, taking him gently by the shoulder.

'You've been through a lot. We all have. But you shouldn't think you did anything wrong.'

Kofi swallowed. There were things he suddenly wanted to say, but he didn't know how.

'Sorry,' he said quietly. It was about all he could manage.

'I just told you you don't need to say that,' replied his brother with a warm smile. 'Mum and Dad are really proud of you, by the way. The way you've been good at school and everything.'

It was true: Kofi had been trying really hard to stay out of trouble. His last report had been the best he'd ever had. Dad even went to the receptionist to check they hadn't put the wrong name on it.

At that point, Gloria came clattering into the front room excitedly, clutching the TV guide in one hand and the phone handset in the other. It was probably Shanice on the other end of the line.

'You lot! *Breakdance the Movie* is on tonight on BBC1! We need to find a tape to—' She paused, interrupting herself. 'What's up?'

'Nothing,' smiled Emmanuel, rising to his feet. 'I was just telling Kofi not to worry. About what happened with Uncle D.'

Now it was Gloria's turn to smile.

'He's right, Kofi,' she said with a wise nod. 'It

must have been so scary. I would have done the same thing as you.'

'Really?' said Kofi, genuinely surprised that his clever-clogs sister thought he wasn't a total idiot.

'Yeah,' Gloria continued. 'You just panicked. But everything worked out in the end. You did well. And Uncle D must be loving those letters you keep writing.'

Kofi smiled in spite of himself.

'Anyway,' said Gloria, putting the handset down and making her way towards the TV cabinet. 'What we gonna tape over to record *Breakdance the Movie*? I vote for ...'

She pulled out a cassette, turned it to one side, and read the label theatrically.

'... Kofi's ... first ... birthday party ... Sounds pretty boring. Let's tape over this one.'

Kofi grinned.

Settled

Apart from the cyphers at school, and the nice talk with his siblings, other things were going well too. With Uncle Delroy being so far away, Jeanette had come back to visit a few times and was really part of the family now. Somehow, she'd even learned how to make a decent brown stew. And even though they were still arguing more than ever, Kofi was glad to be able to talk/argue about music with Gloria. Even better, Shanice's parents had recently got cable TV, which was an extra bonus. She would record all the latest music videos from America, bring the VHS cassette tapes over to watch with Gloria, and they would let Kofi tag along. He'd do ridiculous impressions of US rappers and singers that left the girls falling off the sofa in stitches.

Meanwhile, T from the estate had been given a brand-new Super Nintendo for his birthday and invited Kofi and Kelvin over to play it with his friends Edward the sweet smoker and Patrick with the squint. Kelvin wasn't so excited, but Kofi was blown away by the Super Nintendo's graphics. They looked even better than the arcades. And he didn't have to make fake coins to have a go.

All of these developments had a calming effect on Kofi's life. For the first time he could remember, he felt 'settled'.

And then something very strange happened.

Kofi Starts to Hear Things

It was in the run-up to the holidays, the final couple of weeks before the end of term. Kofi was in the refectory, finishing his lunch with a small group of friends, when he thought he heard a word carry through the air. It wasn't louder than anything else being said, but it was a word he hadn't heard in a while. Not since the tournament days. Not since before Leroy had been suspended from St Campions.

Could it be?

Really?

It sounded just like …

… *Coinboy* …

Kofi stopped mid-sentence and spun his head to hear where it had come from. It was a boy packing up his tray, singing to himself. It was a song that he was half mumbling, half humming to himself. He clearly didn't know all the words, but the melody was clear. Before Kofi could go over to investigate, the boy was gone.

Kofi heard it again after school. He and Kelvin were the only two waiting for a bus heading in the direction of their estates. The bus arrived and the doors slid open. The driver was a youngish, thickset black guy in sunglasses, an open-necked white shirt and a single thin gold chain. Set up on his dashboard was a little radio cassette player, and playing through its tinny speakers was the same melody that Kofi had heard earlier, from that boy at lunchtime.

They stepped on, flashing their bus passes.

'Have you heard that tune before?' Kofi asked Kelvin.

'What tune?' said Kelvin. Then the doors whooshed shut behind them, the song ended, and the moment was gone. Kofi started to wonder if he was beginning to hear things.

But walking through the estate, he heard it again, for the third time that day. This time, it was the bassline he heard first, catching him mid-step on his way towards his block. He'd already said bye to Kelvin. The music was coming from the flat on the top floor: the pirate radio station. Kofi stopped to listen, straining his ears. It was fast and bouncy, full of cluttered drums and a deep, growling bassline. Then the melody kicked in, and it was just like the boy in the refectory was humming, and just like he'd heard on the bus too, but this time he could hear much more definition. Then the lyrics started.

Kofi stopped walking completely.

He gasped.

Then he set off at a sprint towards home.

A Letter from 'Dreaddy D'

'Gloria!' he said, slamming the door shut and shaking his blazer off on to the floor. 'Have you heard that song?'

In a rare moment of sibling telepathy, Gloria knew exactly what Kofi was talking about.

'Yes!' she replied. 'The one that goes...'

And she hummed the melody.

'Yeah, that one! Who is it? It sounds just like—'

They said the next two words in perfect unison.

'*Uncle Delroy!*'

But how?

'Quick, turn on the radio.'

Kofi darted over to the hi-fi and flicked it on, turning slowly through every frequency on the FM dial. There were a lot of pirate stations in and among the proper ones, and he was hoping that one of them might be playing the mystery song.

After a minute or so, the melody fuzzed into being.

'There!' said Gloria.

'Shh!' said Kofi, and she immediately slapped him on the back of the head.

They leaned forward. The lyrics started.

'*Yo.*'

It *was* Uncle Delroy!

The words were fast and skippy and difficult to understand. Kofi had to close his eyes to really concentrate. A few words leaped out at him. '*... money ... police ... estate ...*'

And then, there it was. That word again. Leroy's old nickname for Kofi: '*Coinboy*' ... Or was it '*go-on boy*'? Or something else?

Then the song was interrupted by the voice of the DJ, giving shout-outs to local listeners and saying *hold tight* like a fairground-ride operator.

Kofi stood up, excited and utterly, utterly confused.

How could it be that Uncle Delroy had made a song that was being played on pirate radio?

The front door clacked open and Kofi and Gloria heard someone dropping keys in the bowl before shuffling through the post. Moments later, Emmanuel entered the front room holding a letter. He extended it to Kofi.

'You need to start checking the post,' he said. 'I think it might be from Uncle Delroy.'

Gloria and Kofi looked at each other. Then Kofi grabbed the envelope and tore it open. The other two crowded round to read the letter inside, over his shoulders.

Dear Kofi,

Wha gwan! It's your uncle Delroy. Thank you so much for your letters. I love receiving them and hearing about all the happenins at the flat. Tell Jeanette to stop trying to cook so much. Shes a danger to mankind in that kitchen.

I got some good news for you.

Remember I told you I used to do music back in the day? Well one of the boys I work with got a little studio in a flat up here. I know the producer from way back. We was boys when I was a little yute like you.

Anyway, when you sent me those raps I was realy touched. You got some bars, Kofi! I took them to the studio and we used some of them in a new song Adam been working on. He calls it 'Jungle'. I did my ting, as you might expect from a badboy like me. We made a tape and we might even be able to get a few dubplates made out on road. I know a few soundboys out there who might give it a little spin. You neva know.

I know how much you and your brother and sister love your music so when I'm out I hope you can hear the tune.

Send my love to everyone. I saw that Gladiators and that Shadow is looking a bit shaky shaky and I'm working out NUFF so boy he better watch out!

Peace and love.
Uncle Delroy

Kofi let his hands drop.

'What raps?' he said.

There was a confused silence as the three siblings struggled to piece it all together. Then Gloria clapped a hand on her forehead.

'Last week!' she exclaimed.

'What about last week?' asked Kofi. He turned to Emmanuel. 'What happened last week?'

'Last week, you left one of your letters on the floor by the door, didn't you?' explained Gloria. 'I gave it to Mum to post to Uncle D. It must have been the one with the raps.'

Kofi paused.

'What raps?' he repeated. 'I didn't write any raps.'

Gloria paused.

'So whose letter was that?'

Making Trouble Look Good

The three siblings looked blankly at each other, wondering where on earth a random page of raps might have come from, while the pirate radio station buzzed with static in the background. It would be three whole days until this particular little mystery was solved, when Kelvin quietly asked Kofi if he ever got the poem that he had slid under his door.

Because that's what had happened. Four weeks earlier, when Kofi had made that phone call on the run from the police, Kelvin had actually picked up the line, only Kofi couldn't hear him. He'd heard every word Kofi had said and it had stayed in his mind. He was worried for his friend and wrote about it all that night, in his journal. Being a natural poet, he made it rhyme, and then thought it might be nice to deliver the poem to Kofi's flat. Then Kelvin's poem got posted to Uncle Delroy by accident and that was how Kofi's story ended up being made into a song. What happened next was unbelievable.

No one could have predicted how far Uncle D's song would travel once it touched the underground. Only about a week after Kofi first heard it, it suddenly seemed to be *everywhere*. People were calling it 'Coinboy', because that's what it sounded like Uncle D was saying in the chorus. Kofi quite liked the idea of it being about him, but he didn't even bother trying to tell people that it was his uncle rapping because no one would have believed him. It was like when people said that Ian Wright was their mum's cousin's best friend. Everyone just rolled their eyes.

By the time Uncle D was on his way back home, 'Coinboy' had become a bit of an underground hit. You couldn't buy it in the shops, but it was doing the rounds on bootleg cassette tapes that people were recording at home. It helped that the song came with a mysterious backstory. No one knew who *Commander A* and *Dreaddy D* even were. Kofi wrote long letters to his uncle, telling him all about how well the song was doing and how everyone was talking about Dreaddy D at school.

When he played the song to his parents, it took them a minute to even work out what they were hearing. Dad said he must be getting old and Mum agreed, but when Uncle D's voice rasped into gear with that unmistakable '*Yo*', both their eyes widened like toddlers.

'Is that really Delroy?' asked Mum in disbelief.

'Yep,' beamed Kofi proudly. 'He's talking about me.'

Mum paused for a moment, then smiled as she shook her head.

'He even makes getting in trouble look good ...' she said happily.

And Kofi had to agree.

Epilogue

'Now I didn't quite stick to the recipe,' announced Jeanette as she leaned to turn off the light switch with her nose. 'But I'm pretty sure I've made a *perfect* curry goat lasagne this time.'

Kofi walked ahead of her, carefully carrying a stack of plates towards the foldaway table.

The flat was packed. Most of the sofas were taken and Emmanuel was propped against a wall by the window. Kofi had been helping Jeanette cook while Mum fought every instinct in her body to stay out of the kitchen.

Gloria was setting the table and doing a pretty fantastic job of fitting on all the cutlery and glasses at angles that would have made her maths teacher proud. Her friend Shanice was helping, carefully folding serviettes into little origami swans. The few that could stand up were looking more like dogs than swans.

Shanice would try to set them straight and then cuss them out when they collapsed on the table. She had insisted on coming over if it meant she could actually meet the real Dreaddy D in person. He was coming back to London, and Jeanette had had the idea to throw him a surprise party.

'OK – why do all my swans look like dogs though,' stated Shanice, straightening her back and putting both hands in front of her.

'We used to have a dog,' said Kofi. 'Until, well, you know.' He motioned towards Jeanette's dish.

'Ugh, man,' scowled Shanice, mid-swan. 'I beg someone tell this yute not to joke about them tings.'

'Didn't you used to have a dog back in Jamaica?' Emmanuel asked Mum.

'Still does,' chirped Kofi. 'We call it Glo—'

A cushion hit him smack in the face as mild pandemonium threatened to break out. He couldn't help himself. He was in such a good mood.

The sound of the front door rescued Kofi from being killed by his sister. Everyone went into a hush, with Jeanette patting the air in front of her and saying 'shush' louder than anyone was actually talking. She had really missed Delroy while he had been away.

'SURPRISE!'

Uncle Delroy was momentarily stunned. He entered the front room to an explosion of cheers, hugs and handshakes, followed by Dad, who was clutching a handful of unopened letters. He was still the first person to check the post most days.

Delroy knew everyone in the room and everyone in the room knew him. As cool as he always was, even he had to admit that he was a bit overwhelmed. In a good way. It was a fine homecoming.

The biggest embrace was reserved for Jeanette, who he picked up by the waist and spun around in the air, blowing over four of Shanice's swans in the process. Under normal circumstances Shanice would have kissed her teeth and thrown swan number five on the table. But right now she was too busy trying not to watch *the* Dreaddy D, and blushing secretly.

Uncle Delroy's warmest hug was with Mum. They looked at each other briefly, Mum tilting her head and biting her lip, trying not to cry, before opening both arms.

'Sorry, sis,' said Uncle D into her shoulder. 'Sorry I messed up.'

Mum tried to say, *'It's all right, Delroy,'* but it just came out in a choke of happy tears.

And then:

'What's a *web – site*?'

Dad's voice made everyone stop and quieten down. He was holding a letter and a newly opened envelope. Kofi could tell straight away that it was something to do with money.

'And why am I paying for one?'

There was a sharp intake of breath from somewhere in the room and everyone immediately turned to look at Kofi. He raised both hands in defence. Emmanuel hastily interjected.

'Oh, Dad, listen, I can explain,' he began. 'It's this thing on the internet. I started one up with a friend. But you need a bank account to register.'

Dad raised an eyebrow.

'What's the *inter-net*?' he said.

'I'll pay you back,' Emmanuel continued in a rush. 'I forgot to mention it. Sorry.'

Dad slowly lowered the eyebrow.

'I've heard of the internet,' said Gloria with an air of authority. 'It's like a way you can share information on computers and put things up for people to read.'

'Oooh,' said Jeanette. She had absolutely no idea what anyone was talking about.

'Sounds rubbish,' said Kofi cheerfully. 'I can't believe

you're wasting Dad's money. What's your website called anyway?'

Emmanuel looked around the room.

'*Lyrics dot com*,' he said finally. 'It's a music lyrics page. A few friends are helping me with the design.'

Shanice and Kofi looked at each other.

'Naah,' said Kofi. 'We did that already. It'll never catch on.'

He turned to start serving up some plates.

'Trust me.'

Enjoy a sneak peek at
Kofi's next adventure . . .

KOFI

and the Secret Radio Station

'Ey rudeboy, you wanna go live?'

When Linton said 'live' his eyes widened to show the whites all round and his eyebrows rose up high on his forehead. Kofi mimicked him unconsciously, grinning too. He didn't know what it meant, but it sounded exciting.

Linton started hovering over the equipment, switching buttons that Kofi had already forgotten the purposes of. T watched intently. Then Linton reached into a nearby crate and withdrew a random 12 inch vinyl record with a blank white label. Kofi noticed that the crate had a piece of masking tape on it with the word 'Jungle' written in graffiti scrawl. Linton carefully placed the record on a turntable and lowered the needle with delicate fingers. Then he leaned to the right and pushed a red button with one hand, while flicking two switches with the other.

The red light oozed into life.

Kofi jumped at the sound of the music as the record started playing. It was all clattering drums and a wobbly baseline, filling the flat with sound. Loud. Then the vocals kicked in. Kofi recognised it immediately.

'Coinboy!' he exclaimed.

Take a walk through musical history . . .

A Times Rock and Pop Music Book of the Year

Musical Truth

A Musical Journey through Modern Black Britain

'Fantastic.'
Clash Magazine

'Engaging and accomplished.'
Guardian

JEFFREY BOAKYE

Art by Ngadi Smart